FRIEND OR FOE 3

Mimi

Lock Down Publications and Ca$h
Presents

Friend or Foe 3

A Novel by *Mimi*

Lock Down Publications
P.O. Box 944
Stockbridge, Ga 30281

Visit our website @
www.lockdownpublications.com

Friend or Foe 3

First Edition August 2021
Printed in the United States of America

Lock Down Publications
Like our page on Facebook: Lock Down Publications @
www.facebook.com/lockdownpublications.ldp

Book interior design by: **Shawn Walker**
Edited by: **Nuel Uyi**

Stay Connected with Us!

Text **LOCKDOWN** to 22828 to stay up-to-date with new releases, sneak peaks, contests and more… Thank you.

Submission Guideline

Submit the first three chapters of your completed manuscript to ldpsubmissions@gmail.com, subject line: Your book's title. The manuscript must be in a .doc file and sent as an attachment. Document should be in Times New Roman, double spaced and in size 12 font. Also, provide your synopsis and full contact information. If sending multiple submissions, they must each be in a separate email.

Have a story but no way to send it electronically? You can still submit to LDP/Ca$h Presents. Send in the first three chapters, written or typed, of your completed manuscript to:

LDP: Submissions Dept
Po Box 944
Stockbridge, Ga 30281

DO NOT send original manuscript. Must be a duplicate.

Provide your synopsis and a cover letter containing your full contact information.

Thanks for considering LDP and Ca$h Presents.

Acknowledgements

First and foremost, I always want to shout out God because he knew what he was doing when He made me and gave me this gift. Not everyone can write a book, but He chose me to do so!

Thank you to everyone who has supported me throughout my writing career. In 2015 I became a published author. It has been a long road to get to where I am at now but nonetheless, I am grateful. I have found my place at LDP when I wanted to quit and the response from my releases with each book pushed me to stay the course. It is through them (LDP) and supporters that made me realize that this writing shit won't stop!

To my family: we aren't perfect but we always have each other's back and show support when it counts, and I love y'all for that!

To my other set of family at work: never in a million years did I think that I would have so many people that I didn't know from a can of paint support me the way each and every one of you do! I can't thank y'all enough!

#2275

To everyone who believes in me and pushes me to the max, I love y'all for real!

Enjoy!

Chapter One

Sasha sat on the side of Carmen's bed, looking down at her bandaged friend. From what the doctor had told her, Carmen had burns that covered fifty percent of her body. Most of the damage was to Carmen's body, and a few burns covered her face. According to the police, a neighbor who'd smelled the smoke had called immediately. Thankfully, the firefighters, EMT's, and police got there fast. Carmen's home wasn't burned to the ground, but it was uninhabitable, and repairing it wouldn't be worth the money or time. Sasha felt bad for her friend. While everyone was going through their separate woes, no one thought that Carmen would ever be the victim of a house fire. Sasha couldn't even fathom who would want to bring death to her. When Sasha arrived at the hospital, Carmen was still in surgery, getting skin grafts to the most severe of her burns.

Seeing her girl like this broke her heart. She would never want this for any of her girls. Once she found out who did this, she was going to hunt them down and make sure they spent time in prison for this heinous act. Carmen was the purest of them all and didn't deserve this. Sasha couldn't stand Amekia, but she wouldn't even wish this on her. Sasha sat in the hospital chair by the window, watching the rain cascade down over the city. While she was waiting for Carmen to get out of surgery, she thought about what had happened at her house. Before Jade had called her, Brandon revealed that Nasir was Amekia's brother.

To say that Sasha was surprised was an understatement. Out of all of the years that she had been friends with Amekia, she never knew that she had a brother. *And I end up having an affair with him!* she thought, scolding herself. Had she known that Nasir was related to Amekia in any way, she would have never even picked up his case. When Brandon revealed Nasir was Amekia's brother, the look on Nasir's face told her everything she needed to know. While she was attacking him, the gun had gone off. By the grace of God, she wasn't hit. Nasir, however, shot himself in the thigh. Sasha's mind replayed it in her mind. She knew that she was wrong for leaving him there, but the call she received about Carmen was more important than him. She dressed hurriedly and left the house while Nasir sat on the floor in the dining room, holding a cloth to his wound.

Knock! Knock!

Sasha's thoughts came back to the present, as she swiped fresh tears from her face while the doctor came inside the room. Sasha stood up and extended her hand which the doctor took in hers and shook firmly.

"How is she?" Sasha asked, her voice quivering.

"Her surgery went well. All we have to do is give her body time to heal. Carmen will be sedated for the most part of her stay so that we make sure we get her burns to heal. She will also be in a lot of pain, so we have a direct line of morphine hooked up, and all she has to do is push one button to administrate her medication. The police will want to come and speak with her when she is awake but I have to ask you, do you know anyone who would do this?" The doctor asked with concern written all over her face.

"Dr. Rashesh, I wish I did know. Carmen didn't have any issues with anyone and I'm sure when she wakes up and speaks with the officers, she will fully cooperate. I won't lie, I can't wait until she's up. I'm hoping that she knows who did this so I can make sure I work closely with the DA to get justice for my friend. She didn't deserve this."

Dr. Rashesh understood Sasha completely. She had seen this situation many times, with females either being burned or shot because of a crazy ex. She just prayed that this was an accident. The police suspected foul play, but they didn't know for sure until the fire Marshall did a full investigation. Dr. Rashesh shook Sasha's hand one more time, before she let her know that Carmen will be in her room shortly.

Handing Sasha her card with her cell number on it, Dr. Rashesh said: "If there is anything that I can do for you, don't hesitate to give me a call. Here is my card. Once again, I am really sorry about what happened to Carmen. The police will be in shortly." Sasha displayed a small smile on her face, as she pocketed the card the doctor had given her. Sasha exhaled and took a seat in the chair next to the bed. Her mind swirled with thoughts of who could have done this to Carmen. Her thoughts were interrupted when her phone chimed with a text from Jade.

Jade: How is Carmen?

Sasha: She is out of surgery but the doctor said that they are going to keep her heavily sedated to allow her burns to heal. I can't believe that somebody tried to burn her house down with her in it.

Jade: Did Denise make it there?

Sasha: No. I didn't call her, did you?

Jade: No! Only because I thought you were going to contact her.

Sasha: Dammit! I'm going to call her now... hopefully, she could let us in on something that we don't know because this one right here is bogus. How is it going with Amekia?

Jade: Don't even get me started! She is distraught and I don't know what there is that I could do for her. The police are acting like they don't believe her! They keep side eyeing her! And if they weren't law, I would be setting every one of these motherfuckers straight!

Sasha: Keep me posted! I'm going to try and call Denise and I will let you know if anything changes. The police are here and want to ask me questions.

Jade: Okay. Whisper in Carmen's ear and tell her we all love her and we are praying for her. Tell her that we will get justice for her!

I simply replied to Jade with an *okay*, and closed my phone. Two plain-clothed officers walked into the room with grim expressions on their faces. Sasha stood up and shook each one of their hands and introduced herself. The first detective spoke up, "Mrs. Isaacs, I am truly sorry about what happened to your friend—Miss Bowden. We are going to do all that we can in order to take down the person or persons who are responsible. However, since Miss Bowden is unable to speak with us right now, we would like to ask you some questions to see if that can help us with our investigation."

"Oh yeah, sure. Anything to help out my best friend." The detectives proceeded to ask Sasha questions, and she answered as best she could. Once the detectives were done, Sasha tried calling Denise but ended up getting her voicemail. Sasha looked at her phone with a frown and hung up without leaving a message. She found it odd that Carmen was the only one in the house during the incident, and now Denise wasn't answering. Something was fishy, and Sasha was going to get to the bottom of things. Until then, Sasha made the dreadful phone call to Carmen's mother.

***

Jade watched Amekia pace back and forth in the living room. Amekia was pulling at her hair, talking to herself. Jade couldn't help but to feel bad for her friend. She could see the deep worried lines that etched Amekia's face. She wished she knew what to do to fix the situation. But, as the cops said, there was nothing more they could do. There was an Amber Alert issued, and the detectives were knocking on doors to see if anyone had seen anything. Brandon sat on the love seat at the opposite side of the living room, with his hands on his head.

"Amekia honey, please sit down," Jade said in a smooth voice. She couldn't imagine going through what Amekia was currently going through.

"Jade, I can't fucking sit. I should be out there helping. I should be doing something instead of running a damn hole into my fucking carpet! That is my baby and I can't even begin to think who the fuck would want to fucking take her away!" Amekia yelled. Her eyes were bloodshot and swollen from crying.

"I also don't know who could be behind it, but you walking back and forth in this damn living room ain't going to help. Who do you think is capable of doing something like this? How the fuck anybody get in here if all of the windows and doors were locked?" Jade questioned. She didn't expect answers, yet she asked those questions out loud.

"If I knew, you think that I would be pacing so fucking much!" Amekia shouted.

Brandon jumped in and said, "Mekia babe, Jade just trying to help. We can't do anything except wait for the police to give us an update. When they do, we can ask them what they need for us to do."

"The longer we wait, the further my baby will be. They could be doing anything with her! They could be abusing her! Oh my God! I'm a terrible mother!" Amekia cried out. Brandon stood from the couch, walked up to Amekia, and placed his arms around her. Jade watched as he kissed her on the forehead, assuring her the situation was going to be okay.

Jade saw how Brandon was with Amekia for the first time, and she knew that it wasn't just sex with her best friend. He was in love with her, and from the way Amekia melted into his body, she knew that Amekia felt the same way.

While stroking Amekia's hair, Brandon looked towards Jade. "Um, Jade, it's getting late and I know you had a long day yourself. Go home and get some rest. I will call you if something comes up." Jade nodded in understanding. She was a nervous wreck just sitting there, and a hot shower was calling her name. Jade walked over to Brandon and Amekia, and placed her arms around the two. She didn't want to disturb their hug, so she included Brandon in the hug.

"Amekia, now may not be the time but Sasha told me to tell you if you need anything to let her know," Jade said. Amekia gave Jade a look with a small smile. Her eyes were still bloodshot. She closed her eyes and leaned into Brandon, giving Jade the cue to leave. With a quick nod, Jade made her exit. She headed home to shower and lay down. Before sleeping, she made a mental note to head to the hospital in the morning to check on Carmen.

Chapter Two

Brandon and Amekia must have stayed swaying back and forth in the living room for an hour. He held Amekia in his arms, periodically kissing the top of her forehead. Amekia wanted to do more concerning her daughter's situation, but for the life of her, she couldn't think of a thing that she could really do about the whole thing. For that she felt useless. Amekia took a deep breath, taking the scent of Brandon in, and couldn't help but thank God that Brandon was here at this moment.

"You want some water?" Brandon asked, as he rubbed his hand up and down Amekia's back.

"No." Amekia sniffled. She continued, "I want Aziyah, Brandon. Why the fuck haven't they found her yet!"

"Mekia, they are doing everything they can. I'm pretty sure they are going to find her. We just need to have faith that it will be sooner rather than later."

Ding! Dong! Ding! Dong

The sound of the doorbell rang throughout the house, ceasing the conversation between the two. Amekia pulled away from Brandon, and went to answer the door. On the other side of the door was her brother. She wasn't expecting him, and was surprised that he was there. She looked up at Nasir with sad eyes, and instantly felt like a little girl. She fell into his arms, crying again. Nas smoothed his hand across Amekia's head, shushing her.

"What's wrong? What happened?" Nas asked.

"Somebody took Aziyah!" Amekia bellowed.

"What? What the fuck you mean somebody took my niece? Why didn't you call me when it happened?"

"I didn't have time to call you. And I'm pretty sure that you were with Sasha anyhow and you wouldn't have answered." Amekia wiped her tears away.

Nas squeezed past Amekia, and headed towards the living room. He said over his shoulder, "You don't have to worry about her finding out. Thanks to your boyfriend, she knows."

"Wait, why are you walking with a limp? Did that bitch hurt you?"

"I shot myself, making sure I didn't accidentally shoot her." Nas was going to continue to explain, but he noticed that Brandon was sitting on the couch with his head in his hands. Anger ripped through Nas, as he ran over to the couch and clocked Brandon upside his head with a right hook. Brandon jumped up from the couch, and sent a hard left, right combo to Nas' gut.

"Nigga, what the fuck you think you doing?" Brandon yelled. If his daughter wasn't missing, he would have had Nas all over the living room.

"You were so busy trying to make Sasha miserable, that my fucking niece went missing!" Nas yelled as Amekia came inside the living room, trying to break them up.

"Nas, this is not Brandon's fault. It's mine. I shouldn't have left her alone in her room to shower."

"Do you hear yourself! How can you blame yourself for that shit! You needed to shower!" Brandon yelled. He was going to make sure that Amekia didn't blame herself. She was already a wreck, and placing blame on herself didn't go down well with Brandon. The room got quiet as they looked at each other.

"Wait. Nas, you said that Brandon was too busy trying to make Sasha miserable, what did you mean?" Amekia asked. Brandon looked at her with a crazy look. Their daughter was missing, yet she was focusing on something that didn't need attention.

Nas answered, "That isn't what we need to be focusing on right now, Mekia. We need to put our heads together and see how we can get Aziyah back. Better believe who fucking did this is getting dealt with."

Brandon caught the shade that Nas threw his way, but one thing was for sure, Nas didn't have to worry about Brandon being the mastermind behind his daughter's abduction. Besides, there was no need to stage a kidnapping when Amekia was willing to allow him to see Aziyah whenever he wanted to. Brandon shook his head and headed to the kitchen to grab Amekia a bottle of water, and to give her time to bring her brother up to speed. *When this blows over and I get my baby girl back, I'm gonna body this nigga!* Brandon thought to himself, eyeing Nas from the door of the living room.

Amekia woke up the next morning with a pounding headache. She didn't remember climbing into the bed, but she was thankful that's where she woke up. Amekia didn't mean to get drunk, but Nas had said that it would take the edge off. She remembered one drink turning into another, and soon after, she was taking shots. Nas ended up leaving, telling his sister that he was going to try to speak with Sasha. He was, in fact, going to round up some of his people to shake up some of the neighborhoods. To see if anybody knew anything.

Amekia sat up in bed with her hands on her head. The room was spinning, and the urge to throw up tickled the back of her throat. Brandon sat on the edge of the bed, a mug of coffee in his hands, watching Amekia. Amekia gagged, and next thing she knew, she was hugging the toilet, with Brandon standing at the door.

"You need to put something in your stomach," Brandon stated. Amekia rolled her eyes as her throat burned from the bile.

"Brandon, did you hear anything from the police?" She managed to croak out. Her throat was raw.

"No. I called this morning to see if there was anything new. The only thing is that now the FEDS are on the case. Can you please put something in your stomach? You need to soak up that liquor you consumed last night."

"Brandon, I can't eat. I don't have an appetite." Amekia whined as she leaned into the toilet bowl a little more, her stomach caving in as she felt like she was going to throw up some more. *Ain't shit else in my stomach, what the fuck is going to come up? My intestines?* Amekia thought to herself.

"Get up," Brandon said with authority. He knew what Amekia was feeling because it involved his child, but they were no good to Aziyah if they weren't at their greatest. Amekia tried to protest, but Brandon grabbed her by her arm and picked her up.

"Brandon, no!" Amekia cried. She continued with tears streaming her face, and snot bubbles forming in her nostrils, "I can't do this!"

Brandon let Amekia go. As he did that, he pushed her arm a bit, causing her to stumble a little. Brandon threw the mug that he had in his hand against the hallway wall behind him, causing Amekia to stop her crying and look at him like he was crazy. Eyes bulging, his finger pointed in her face, Brandon yelled, "You need to get your shit together! You think I don't know how you are feeling about this? She is my child too, and my heart is breaking at the thought of me not being able to do anything! You think I want to be sitting here looking lost while the FEDS are out searching for my baby girl and not doing anything? Huh! Get your shit together,

Amekia, and let's work together on figuring out how we gonna get Aziyah back!"

Brandon was through with Amekia. He got her actions, but that shit wasn't getting them anywhere. The next best thing was for them to come up with a strategy on how to get their daughter. After his outburst, Brandon needed to get some fresh air. He left Amekia looking on in shock as she stood in the middle of the hallway. When Amekia heard the door slam, she slowly made her way inside of her bedroom, thinking about what Brandon said. She admitted to herself he was right. She needed to be stronger for her baby girl, and at that moment she vowed that she would.

Ring! Ring! Ring!

Amekia's phone rang and vibrated on the dresser. The last thing she wanted was to answer a phone call that didn't have anything to do with Aziyah. Sniffling, she reached for her phone. Through her puffy eyes, she didn't recognize the phone number. She debated whether to answer. Before she realized it, the caller hung up. Moving to place her phone on her dresser, the phone rang in her hand, the screen displaying the same number.

"Hello?" Amekia answered, her voice filled with skepticism.

"Amekia?" The caller questioned, instantly leaving a bad taste in her mouth.

"Mama? What the fuck do I owe for this phone call?" Amekia asked in a venomous tone. Her face bunched up in disgust.

"You watch the tone that you take with me—I am still your mother and you will respect me," Mrs. Lewis replied.

"Now you want to call yourself a mother? Last time I checked, a mother is supposed to protect her child at all costs, but all you did was push me into a fire that I will never forgive you for."

There was a short pause before Mrs. Lewis spoke. She said, "That is exactly why I am calling. I have made some mistakes with you, and I want to correct them. You are right. A mother is supposed to protect her child, and that is all that I was trying to do with you."

"You cannot be serious right now! You allowed that man to violate my body in the most indescribable way! I called for your help! You did nothing to help me! You smiled after he raped me, and you did nothing!"

"Greg was going to be your husband, Amekia. You ran away as soon as you felt what sex was like, and spread your legs for every Tom, Dick, and Harry you came across! All Greg wanted to do was, take care of you."

Fire danced through Amekia's veins as she listened to what delusional bullshit her mother was spitting. She was disgusted. Having her mother admit to her wrongdoing was a waste of her time. She needed to join the hunt in finding her daughter.

"As much as I want to go down memory lane and beat your ass for the shit that you put me through, I got more important shit to tend to. Do not call me again unless you want to catch these hands."

"Wait a minute, Amekia! I know there is bad blood between us but let me tell you that where I failed you, I will now do for your daughter. You already began her life messed up by having her with a married man, but I can correct that over the years and groom her to what you were supposed to be."

Amekia's heart hammered in her chest as she listened to Aziyah's cries before the phone hung up. She felt light-headed before she exhaled a bloodcurdling scream. Brandon heard the scream from the porch, and instantly ran into the house. He ran up to Amekia's room, where he saw her leaning against the wall with her hand on her stomach, her cell phone on the floor.

"Amekia, what's wrong?" Brandon asked, as he tried to think of what made Amekia scream the way that she did. Amekia's breath was stuck in her throat as her thoughts raced.

"My-my-my mother has Aziyah," she stammered.

"What? How do you know that?" Brandon asked. He didn't understand why her mother would kidnap her own grandchild.

"I just got off of the phone with her when I heard Aziyah's cries in the background. How could I be so stupid and not suspect her first?"

"Wait a minute, Amekia. Why would your mother want to kidnap her own grandchild? Are you sure?"

"Brandon, I know what Aziyah cries sound like. My mother said that she was going to make up for the failure I became by raising Aziyah. Oh my God! She's going to pimp out my baby! Brandon, instead of standing there, call the damn police." Amekia felt like her heart was shredding into tiny pieces. As Brandon made the call to the detective that was working with the FBI, Amekia picked up the phone and tried dialing the number back. The line didn't go through which only made her heart beat in her chest harder.

"Detective Palumbo is on the way with Agent Williams," Brandon stated, and walked to wrap his arms around Amekia. Instead of fighting him, she melted into his chest. Anger overtook Amekia as her body shook all over.

"I am going to kill this bitch. You hear me, Brandon? This is the last straw for me."

"I know, babe. Let's just take the right steps to get this done. We are going to get Aziyah back. But right now, more than anything, I need for you to keep your head in the game and focus. No one knows what you are going through internally besides me. I am going to be here every step of the way." Brandon reassured Amekia. Amekia was drained and had no more words for the situation. She just wanted her little girl back. Brandon let Amekia go, and she instantly went to shower and be presentable for when the detective and agent got there. The gloves were now off, and she was ready to fight the hardest fight she would endure in her lifetime.

Chapter Three

Jade, after leaving Amekia's house the night before, drove around Schenectady for a few hours, trying to piece together everything that was going on: Carmen laid up in the hospital, in a medically induced coma because she suffered third-degree burns on fifty percent of her body, her goddaughter was missing, Sasha and Brandon were no longer together, and her HIV positive ex plaything tried to rape her. As she drove, she prayed for herself and her best friends, hoping for better days.

After a restless night of tossing and turning, Jade woke up the next morning to someone ringing her doorbell. The headache that throbbed caused her to snap her eyes shut when she opened them. She figured that if she laid there, whoever was ringing her doorbell would get the hint and leave. Not even wishful thinking was going to work in that notion. The doorbell made her head throb more, until she threw the covers back and rushed to the door, ready to curse out whoever came to plague her with the bothersome pressing of the doorbell. As she left the room, she grabbed her burgundy Terry cloth robe, and placed it over her body as she flew downstairs to open the door.

Swinging the door open, she yelled, "You want to lay off my fucking bell!"

Timothy stood in front of Jade with his hands up in the air at his chest. When Jade realized who it was, her face softened, and she tightened the bands on her robe. Out of self-consciousness, Jade's hand flew up to her head to pat down her hair. Luckily, she remembered to place her scarf and bonnet on her head the night before.

"Whoa! Good morning, beautiful—I only rung your bell twice but I do apologize for it to be too early," Timothy stated. He placed his hands in his pockets, while Jade shamelessly ogled this man. He stood at six feet six inches next to her five-foot five-inch frame. He was stocky but in a muscular kind of way. His skin glowed as the morning sun bounced against his medium-brown complexion. His beard glistened, and his waves were on spin.

"Good morning. Maybe it's because of this terrible headache I have that caused the bell to annoy me. What can I do for you?" Jade questioned.

"I got a call from a detective from the Special Victims Unit down at the station. They were trying to get in touch with you, but your phone was going straight to voicemail. They thought that I was your live-in boyfriend and called me to let you know that they would like to speak with you." Timothy's deep voice did something to her.

"Well, shit, why didn't they just come here?"

"I don't know about that but they want to speak with me as well. I figured that we could kill two birds with one stone by coming to get you."

Jade looked at Timothy suspiciously. With his hands in his pockets, he tried to act coy. Jade thought it was cute. With a smile on her face, she said, "I'm going to put some coffee on, would you like to come in and have a cup while I get ready?"

Timothy raised his eyebrows. He was more than ready to wait in his car, but it was hot as hell out and the cool air that was coming from Jade's house helped him make up his mind. He said, "Yeah, sure. If that's not putting you out of your way, of course."

"No, it's no problem—I'll only be half an hour tops," Jade responded. She opened the door wider, and allowed him to come in. As he walked past, she caught a whiff of his cologne. She had smelled many fragrances, and can usually pinpoint the smells, but this one she didn't recognize; nevertheless, she was pleased that it smelled good. Jade padded her way into the kitchen with Timothy on her heels.

"Are you doing okay? Did your friend get her baby back? How's your friend in the hospital?" Timothy asked, taking a seat at the table.

A smile formed on Jade's face. She liked that he asked about her friends. Filling the coffee pot up with water, she replied, "I'm doing okay considering the circumstances. Amekia didn't get Aziyah back yet. I don't even think she heard anything yet. Carmen, I could only assume, is doing okay. After I'm done at the police station, I'm racing right on over to the hospital."

Timothy nodded in understanding as Jade moved around the kitchen, grabbing cups, sugar, and creamer. She placed everything on the table, thanked him for asking, and excused herself to get ready. She bathed in *SheaMoisture African Black Soap Body Wash*, before she stepped out to lotion her body with Dr. Teal's Milk and Honey lotion. She racked her brain on what to wear. *This isn't a date, what the fuck am I doing?* she thought to herself. She rushed into the closet, and picked out a pair of white linen shorts that stopped mid-thigh, a navy-blue tank top, black belt, and a pair of slip-on open-toe flat sandals.

Rushing into the kitchen, Jade grabbed a traveling coffee cup, and made herself some coffee. Timothy looked on with a smile on his face as he inhaled her intoxicating scent.

"What? What are you looking at? You ready, right? Let's go," Jade said, taking a sip of coffee.

Timothy let a rumble of laughter escape his mouth as he replied, "Your bonnet is still on your head."

Embarrassment washed over Jade's face, as she rushed off to the bathroom. She took her bonnet and scarf off. As she made sure her silk wrap was nice and neat, she laughed at herself and made her way back to the kitchen, where Timothy was waiting with her traveling coffee cup in his hand. Jade grabbed her purse and cell phone on the table, and they headed to the police station.

When they arrived, they were whisked away to go speak to Detective Wendell in the Special Victims Unit. Jade was embarrassed and timid at first, but then she began to think about women that he could have done this to. She could put a stop to Darion and save other women's lives. She laid her soul bare, and explained her failed relationship with Darion to the detective. Timothy recounted his involvement to the detective, and when it got hard for Jade to speak, he was there holding her hand. Two hours and several questions later, they were walking out of the Schenectady Police Station.

Jade stopped Timothy before they got back inside his car. She said, "Thank you. You don't know me from a can of paint and you made sure that I was good today, and I don't even know where I would begin to show my appreciation."

Timothy looked at Jade with a smile on his face. He didn't know what it was about this woman, but he wanted to protect her. To be there for her. He sensed that she was a good person, and he just wanted to be there. Finally, he replied, "You can take me on a date as a 'thank you'."

Jade wasn't expecting Timothy to say that and right after he did, she swallowed hard. She said, "You know what? I think that I could make that happen. Let me check up on my friends and I can reach out to you when I'm free."

"I like the sound of that. But don't try to flake, I know where you live."

Jade laughed, as she passed him her cell phone. She said, "Put your number in. I will text you with my number. So, you know, you won't have to come banging my door down."

That caused Timothy to laugh as he punched his number into her cell phone. When he gave her the phone back, she opened the Uber app to call for a car. Before she confirmed it, Timothy took the phone out of her hands. She looked at him with bewilderment in her eyes.

"I took you away from your car, so at least let me take you to your next destination," Timothy said, taking his bottom lip into his mouth.

"Okay," Jade replied with a smirk on her face. Timothy grabbed Jade's hand, and led the way to his car.

When Timothy dropped Jade off, she promised that she would hit him up once she had settled in and made sure that everything was okay with her friends. Dread filled Jade's heart, as she walked inside of the hospital. After grabbing her visitor pass from the front desk, she made her way up to the burn unit in Albany Memorial Hospital.

"How can I help you?" the nurse asked from behind the nurses' station.

"Hi, my sister—Carmen Bowden—was brought in the other day with burns from a house fire," Jade stated.

"Yes. Your sister—Sasha—mentioned that more of her sisters would be coming. Right outside of her door are sterilized gowns, gloves, shoe covers, and hair cap. Put those on before you enter her room. Make sure you wash your hands first." The nurse addressed Jade in a pleasant voice while shuffling papers around. Jade nodded and did what the nurse explained. Pulling the sliding door open, Jade crept into the room timidly. Her breath was caught in her throat as she moved closer to the bed.

"Oh Carmen!" Jade cried out when she saw her best friend. She was hooked to a heart monitor, bandages covered her body, and an oxygen mask rested on her face. The tears fell from Jade's eyes, as she took in the sight before her. Carmen's hands rested against the sides of her body. Carmen's hands were only part of her body that Jade could see that didn't have bandages on. Carefully, she placed her hand on top of Carmen's, and squeezed just the slightest.

"Carmen, we are going to find out who did this. I put that on everything I love. You didn't deserve this." Even though Carmen couldn't respond, Jade knew that her girl was in there somewhere listening. Jade grabbed the chair that was against the wall, and took a seat. Jade took the liberty in telling Carmen everything that was going on. Just because Carmen was in a coma didn't mean that she didn't need to know what was going on. For two hours, Jade had a one-sided conversation with Carmen. When she was done, Sasha waltzed in, dressed in the same get-up that Jade was in.

"Hey, Skank," Sasha said with a smile hidden under her mask.

"Hey, Bitch." Jade replied with her own smile.

"I was actually talking to Carmen, but hey to you too bitch," said Sasha.

"Fuck you," Jade replied with a laugh.

"How long have you been here?" Sasha asked.

Jade looked down at her cell phone, surprised that so much time had passed. Jade said, "Shit, two hours. I didn't know that it was that much time that flew."

"You must have been running your mouth." Sasha laughed. She continued, "Have you heard anything from Amekia?"

Jade shook her head with a sad expression on her face. She said, “No. Last night when I left, Amekia was losing her shit! I could only imagine what she is going through.”

“Shit, who you telling? If anything happens to Alexis and Aliana, I’d lose my mind. I’m going to get in touch with my connect down at the police station to see what is going on. Besides that, how are you? Are you okay?”

“Yeah. I’m okay. There was a detective that wanted to speak with me this morning. Timothy came over and stayed with me every step of the way. Told his side of the story and everything.”

Sasha scrunched up her face at the name she just heard. She asked, “Who the hell is Timothy?”

Jade sucked her teeth and replied, “How are you a lawyer if you can’t put a face to the name? Remember the guy who was there when Darion attacked me? That’s Timothy.”

“Oh, yeah. So that’s why you smiled when you said his name. Ooh! Jade like somebody.” Sasha teased.

“He's cool and all but I don’t know.” Jade shrugged.

“What you mean you don’t know?”

“My situation changes everything about dating. I’m on the fence with taking somebody seriously.”

Sasha grabbed Jade’s hand and squeezed it. She said, “He already knows your status, and he didn’t run off yet. Get to know that man, and take it one day at a time. Just because you are HIV positive doesn’t mean that it’s the end of the world. Give him a chance, Jade.”

Jade soaked up what Sasha said, and nodded. Sasha was right. Jade said, “If this shit doesn't work, bitch, it’s on.”

Sasha threw her head back and laughed at Jade. Meanwhile, Carmen heard everything that was being said. She was trying her hardest to wake up, move a finger or something. But nothing worked. Her body was achy all over. At times, her body still felt like it was burning, like she was still on fire. All she wanted was to wake up.

Chapter Four

It was ten at night when Sasha arrived at her home. The babysitter was sitting on the couch, watching the earlier seasons of *Love and Hip Hop: Atlanta.* Her girls were sleeping soundly in their bedrooms. Sasha paid her babysitter and sent her on her way. Walking into the kitchen, Sasha went into the cup cabinet, and grabbed a glass to fill it with ice. It was a long day, and all she wanted was to sip slowly on a glass of Johnnie Walker Black Label. Adding just the right amount of Coca-Cola, Sasha made her way to the living room. Just as she was getting comfortable, somebody was at her front door, ringing the doorbell.

Exhaling, Sasha got up from the couch and looked through the peephole. Her eyes rolled to the back of her head when she realized who it was. She unlocked the locks, and Nasir stood there in blue jeans, a black and gold Versace t-shirt, all-black Air Max 95's, and a black du-rag on his head. He looked good standing there in his bow-legged stance, eye-fucking Sasha.

"You not gonna let me in?" Nas asked.

"Why should I after the shit you pulled? How could you not tell me Amekia was your sister?" Sasha asked with disappointment etched in her tone.

"She asked me not to. And granted that's not an excuse—"

Sasha cut him off and asked, "Were you fucking with me as some sort of joke? Like did y'all plan to move me out of the picture so that Amekia could get with Brandon behind my back?"

Nas felt like shit that she was thinking that way. His feelings for Sasha were true. He could admit that it wasn't supposed to happen, but he couldn't help but fall for her.

Sasha was everything his deceitful wife wasn't. Sasha didn't take shit, and he needed that in his life.

"Can you let me in so we could talk?" Nas asked, folding his hands in front of him.

"My kids are home. So, no, you can't come in. However, we can sit on the steps and have a conversation. Let me just go inside and grab me my drink." Sasha looked askance at him. As much as she didn't want him there, she needed to hear what he had to say to determine how she wanted to proceed with whatever it was she had with him. When she had her drink in her hand, she slid her feet into a pair of super plush soft house slippers, and she went outside. Nas was leaning against his car when she came back out to sit on the steps.

"Can we at least sit in my car, Sasha? It's hot as hell out here." Nasir was right. Even though the sun went down over two hours ago, it was still humid and dry.

"Fine," Sasha simply replied. Nas moved over to the passenger side of his car, and opened the door for Sasha to slide in. His car smelled of Black Ice mixed with his Tom Ford Black Orchid cologne. Sasha took a long sip from her drink, and placed it in the cup holder as she watched Nas walk to the driver side and climb in. He had Spotify playing softly in the background. A playlist of all of the songs he could think of that reminded him of Sasha. Nas had it bad for this woman, and he needed her to know that.

"You wanted to talk, why you ain't talking?" Sasha asked.

Nas didn't say anything because he didn't know where to begin. He turned in his seat and looked at Sasha, her brown skin glowing under the light from the side of the house. He said, "I wanted to tell you that Mekia was my sister, but knowing the circumstances that y'all was going through, I didn't think that it was the right time to tell you."

"Nas, you gave me all that stuff to show me that Brandon was fucking with Amekia, why do that if she's your sister?" Sasha asked. She needed to know.

Nas was torn between telling Sasha the truth and protecting his sister. Amekia gave him all of that information to give to Sasha because she wanted Brandon to herself. At the time, that's what Amekia wanted, but quickly had a change of heart when Brandon showed signs that he wasn't going to leave his wife. That was until Brandon found out about Nas. Brandon was prepared to fight for his family, and fight the feelings that he had for Amekia until he found out about Nas. To Brandon, that was a sign for him to move forward.

"See you playing games and I am not about to be out here for nothing," Sasha replied, as she grabbed her glass and moved to open the door. Nas grabbed Sasha's arm to stop her from getting out of the car, which caused him to receive a vicious slap to his face.

"Sasha, that was uncalled for," Nas replied calmly, biting on his bottom lip to stop himself delivering the same vicious blow.

"Keep your hands to yourself and I'll do the same."

"You right." For a moment, he thought about how Amekia was going to feel. He was in love with Sasha. If being in love with her meant to have his sister angry with him, then so be it.

"It was her plan. She wanted Brandon for herself and thought that by giving you the proof, it would work in her favor. But when you served her those papers, she knew that pursuing Brandon wasn't the best plan, and she left it alone."

Sasha couldn't believe what she just learned. Amekia was a sheep in wolf's clothing, and had everybody fooled.

Sasha shook her head at how gullible she had been. She knew there was something about Amekia for years that didn't sit well with her, but she could never pinpoint it. Even though she felt something wasn't true with Amekia, Sasha always let that feeling nag at her in the back of her mind.

"I know that's your sister, but I knew for a long time that she was shady. And I kept ignoring that feeling and now look, the bitch got a baby from my husband."

"I know how fucked up this whole situation is, but you have to know that my intentions were never to hurt you. My part in everything was fucked up and as a man I can own up to that. In the process of everything, I fell hard for you, Sasha, and I think that should count for something. Hell, I'm not even holding you accountable for this bullet wound on my thigh."

Sasha's mouth dropped open in shock. She couldn't believe that he would try to even go that route. She said, "One thing for sure, Nasir, you got me two ways fucked up if you think you're gonna hold me accountable for something you did. I wish—"

Nasir placed his finger across her lips, silencing her instantly. Her eyes bugged out of her head, and she looked at him like he was crazy. Nasir said, "Sasha, it was just a joke. The only thing you took from that was that I blamed you for shooting me. Just typical of a woman to pick and choose what it is she wants to hear."

"It ain't even a bullet wound, you got grazed but you're acting like it's the end of the world." Sasha sassed, guzzling the last bit of her drink.

Nasir sighed. She was selecting what it was that she wanted to hear, and it was slowly pissing him off.

"Sasha, you can't—" Nasir started, but stopped when Sasha cut him off.

"I need another drink. This is all too much for me."

"So what? You want to throw what we have down the drain? Just everything?"

"Nasir, what we have is built on lies—"

Nasir looked at Sasha with a wild look in his eyes. Not hatred or hurt, but passion was behind the light in his eyes. He said, "Maybe that's how it started but my feelings for you are real, Sasha. I wish this would have started in a different manner. Look, dammit, Sasha, this is the cards we were dealt with! I want to be your man but you gotta let me be that for you if you have the same feelings that I do."

Sasha looked at Nas with sadness in her eyes. She couldn't comprehend her feelings that she had for him because even though Brandon had done her wrong, she still loved her husband. Everything in her body screamed to divorce Brandon, but her heart told her to fight.

A single tear dropped from Sasha's eye as she said, "Nasir, I gotta go."

"Dammit, Sasha, don't do this. Give us a chance." Nasir wasn't above being vocal about his feelings. He felt strongly for Sasha, and he wanted it to work.

"Have a good night," Sasha said, as she climbed out of his car. Sasha wiped her face of the lone tear, and went inside her house. Sasha immediately went inside her kitchen and made herself a drink. *Why would you want to walk away from him and work something with Brandon and he clearly is the one who would betray you?* Sasha thought to herself. She downed that drink, and made another one, making her way to her bathroom to soak in the tub. Her heart and mind were in a battle, and she needed them to be in one accord.

***

Brandon, with the weight of the world on his shoulders, walked into the house that he shared with his wife. She had texted him, asking him to come over, letting him know that she needed to speak with him. It had been a long day for him and Amekia. The FEDS had made a move on Amekia's mother's house, but when they got there, the house was bare and there was no trace of Mrs. Lewis or Aziyah.

When the door was closed behind him, he leaned against the door with his eyes closed. He had just left Amekia at her house, and he was exhausted. He convinced her to take a Valium that he had gotten from his mother, and it worked wonders by putting her to sleep, allowing him to leave to see what Sasha wanted.

The sounds of her heels clicking against the hardwood floor jarred his eyes open. The foyer where he stood was dark, but the kitchen light was on and it illuminated her frame. Turning the foyer light on, he saw Sasha dressed in a light pink lace bralette and pantie set. Completing the ensemble were light pink thigh-high stockings with the matching garter belt attached. On her feet were six-inch pink, red bottom pumps. Her hair, a twenty-six-inch jet-black lace front, reached down her back. Brandon's mouth dropped open as he watched Sasha slowly make her way to him. He could smell the perfume—Bright Crystal by Versace—that she sprayed on before she left her room. His dick grew in his pants, as much as he tried to fight it.

"Thank you for coming, Brandon," Sasha cooed as she passed about five feet in front of him.

"W-what did you want to talk about? Are the girls okay?" Brandon stammered as he ogled her body.

"Why don't you have a seat on the couch? The girls are okay. They are sleeping soundly."

Brandon moved over to the couch, and sat down. He could hear Sasha approaching him slowly, as he wondered what game she was playing. The last time they spoke, she was dead set on divorcing his black ass but now, here she was; dressed in next to nothing, wanting to talk about only-God-knows-what.

"So what is it you want to talk about? Last I remembered, you told me that you wanted a divorce and you seemed like you were dead set on that. If the girls are good, what do you need to talk about?" Brandon questioned as he watched Sasha stand in front of him.

"I have been thinking. I know I should be done with you for doing the unforgivable but you are my husband. Sometimes we have to sacrifice some things in a marriage and work it out. And on the strength of having your children, that is what I want to do. We can fix this and move on and never speak on this hiccup ever again."

"But Sasha—"

Sasha cut Brandon off and straddled his lap. She took his face into her hands, and placed a kiss on his lips. His hands instantly grabbed her ass cheeks. There was a hint of mint on her breath as well as whatever liquor she had that night. Sasha ground her hips, pushing her pussy against his hard dick through his pants. This wasn't what he came over for, and Sasha wasn't making it easy. She grabbed his hand and placed it on the crotch of her panties, making her clit throb. Against his better judgment, Brandon slid the fabric from her pussy, and slid his fingers over her wetness.

"That feels good, baby," Sasha moaned against Brandon's lips. She moved her body back closer to his knees, and grabbed at his belt. She began to unbutton his pants to free his dick. Brandon's hands hastily moved up and down Sasha's back every so often, gripping her ass cheeks.

Sasha took his shirt off, displaying his muscular arms, chest, and abs. His torso showed off his tattoos, including his newest one. It was Aziyah's name over his heart. For a moment, it gave Sasha a pause, but she shook it off and got her mind together. Brandon reached up and around Sasha's back, unhooking her bra. Her C-cup spilled over and caused Brandon to salivate. He was using both of his hands and pushing her breasts together, his tongue flicking over her nipples. Sasha arched her back, and moved her hips to grind against his rock-hard erection.

Sasha slid off of Brandon's lap, and stood in front of him. Leaving her shoes on, she turned around and pulled her panties down, showing her perfectly apple-shaped ass. She looked at Brandon over shoulder, and bit her bottom lip. Brandon had lifted the lower half of his body to pull his pants down to his ankles. He still had his boxers on, but his dick was poking through the hole, and he was slowly stroking himself. Sasha walked back over to him, and squatted in front of him, removing his hands from his dick and replacing them with hers. Gathering up spit in her mouth, she let it drop down onto his tip to lubricate while she used her hands to stroke his hardness. Brandon's head fell back against the couch, and his eyes closed.

"Damn, Sasha!" He moaned in a whisper. He couldn't remember the last time he dipped his dick into something wet, and he felt relaxed in her hands. Sasha leaned closer to him, and placed him in her mouth. Squeezing her jaws around his length, she maneuvered her head up and down his shaft, making sure his dick was coated well with her saliva. She felt the stickiness in between her legs as her juices leaked from her pussy. The light moans that escaped his mouth caused her to bob her head up and down faster. Brandon's toes curled, as the tip of his dick touched the back of her throat. Sasha took his dick out of her mouth, making a popping sound with the head of his dick, dripping saliva. She licked the bottom of his shaft from the back, starting at the tip. She massaged his balls with the tips of her fingers, before she stuck her tongue out and swirled it around his sack. Brandon's eyes bulged out of his head in surprise. All of the years they had been together, and Sasha never put his balls in her mouth.

"Mmm!" Sasha moaned on his sack.

"Fuck, Sasha!" Brandon moaned. She was stroking his dick as she softly sucked on his balls, causing his eyes to roll to the back of his head. When she came up for air, there was a lazy smile on her face, and her chin was wet. She leaned back onto her elbows, and spread her legs open. She used her index and middle finger to push her folds back and rubbed her clit in small circles. Lying on her back, she used her free hand to beckon Brandon to her. Brandon reached down to his pants, and went into his wallet to get a condom. When Sasha heard him fumbling with the wrapper, she wanted to curse him out. They never used condoms, but the common sense side of her understood why he was using the condom. After all, she had been fucking his baby mother's brother and for all she knew, he was still fucking her.

When Brandon had the condom secured, he got comfortable between her legs and entered her, the sound of her wetness filling the room. Brandon used one of his hands to hold her arms over her head, and began deep-stroking her. Her legs instantly wrapped around his waist, as she moaned out in pleasure. Brandon bit down on his bottom lip, remembering just how good and gushy his wife's pussy was. He almost slid out and took the condom off. The split second that he thought about her fucking on Nasir made him keep the condom on.

Brandon made the mistake of letting her hands go, and she immediately began clawing away at his back, and he regretted it almost immediately. His back was on fire, so he paused and slid out of her, instructing her to flip over and put her ass in the air. Sasha had the perfect arch, causing Brandon to admire her ass for a second. He entered her, while balancing himself on the balls of his feet, and holding onto her waist. Her moans and the sound of her ass smacking against his pelvis filled the air.

“We're gonna have to continue this upstairs if you can’t be quiet. You're gonna wake the girls up.” Brandon fussed. Sasha agreed, and they made their way upstairs to the bedroom that they used to share. Brandon continued to stroke himself as he made his way up the stairs. Inside of the room, Sasha turned music on loud enough to drown out her moans. Brandon locked the door and directed Sasha to get back in the doggy style position on the bed. He climbed back on top of her, his right knee planted on the bed, his left foot planted and bent at the knee. He inserted himself, and placed his hands on her waist. Brandon coached Sasha to throw her ass back, and she complied, her hands grabbing at the pillows and sheets as Brandon dug into her deep.

“Oh my God, Brandon! I’m gonna cum.” Sasha moaned.

“Mmhm, cum on that dick,” Brandon coached from behind. He moved his hips at an angle, feeling himself ready to cum. Sasha was calling on Jesus, as he felt her squirting. He knew that he was hitting her spot; it was the only way that she would squirt. Keeping his pace, he reached under her, and rubbed her clit as he brought her back to another orgasm. As he tried to stay in while she squirted, he grunted out of pleasure. It turned him on when she did that shit, driving him crazy. Brandon felt that familiar sensation, and tapped Sasha on her thigh. She immediately turned onto her back, and watched Brandon snatch the condom off and stand over her. He jerked his dick until his kids erupted, landing on her face and chest. Sasha had a smirk on her face, as Brandon collapsed onto the bed. His breathing was heavy, and he just wanted to regain it only to fall asleep shortly after.

***

"Daddy!" Brandon heard his daughters yelling his name. His eyes flew open just as he felt them jump onto their mother's bed.

"Good morning, my babies," Brandon said with a smile. He had missed waking up to their faces, and he knew that they did too. He figured that Sasha told them he was here.

'Daddy, are you coming back home?" his oldest daughter—Alexis—asked. He knew he should have just left last night. He didn't want to lie to his daughters, but he also had a feeling that Sasha had something to with it.

"Is your mom in the kitchen cooking?" he asked instead.

"Yes," they answered in unison.

"Can y'all go down and help her and let daddy brush his teeth? I'll be right there."

"Yay!" They yelled and made their way out of the room. Brandon ran his hand down his face because this was the last thing he wanted to go through. Getting out of the bed, he looked in the closet and found some of his old clothes in a duffel bag. His clothes were still downstairs from the night before, and he was glad that he left that bag in the back of the closet.

As he made his way downstairs, he could smell the aroma of bacon being cooked, along with coffee brewing. His daughters were sitting at the table, coloring in their coloring books. Sasha stood at the kitchen counter, cutting potatoes into bite-sized pieces on top of a cutting board. When she felt his presence, she walked over to where he stood, and wrapped her arms around his waist, trying to plant a kiss on his lips. At the last moment, Brandon turned his head, and her lips landed on his cheek. She pulled away, and looked at Brandon questioningly.

"We need to talk," Brandon simply said while motioning his head towards the living room. He made his way towards the living room as Sasha made the girls a quick bowl of cereal. She took the bacon off of the burner, and followed Brandon into the living room.

"What is it that we need to talk about?" Sasha asked with a concerned look on her face.

"You told or hinted to the girls that I was coming back?" Brandon asked, trying to keep his voice low.

"Well, yeah. Was I not supposed to?" Sasha was confused. She'd thought that because they fucked like rabbits and he'd spent the night, things were back to normal.

"No. Why would you? Do you think because we had sex last night, that meant that we were getting back together?" Brandon questioned.

"Yes."

"That is not what that meant, Sasha."

"So why would you fuck me?" She was now beginning to get upset.

"You were throwing it at me. I thought you wanted to talk to me about something important and you willingly gave up the pussy."

"You are my husband, Brandon, and I am willing to fight for this marriage."

Brandon chuckled and responded, "Sasha, you out here fucking your ex-best friend's brother who just so happen to be a nigga that you was defending. Why would I come back home? Why would I want to make it work? You were just so dead set on divorcing me."

"And you're a saint? You fucked my best friend and got her pregnant. If I'm willing to forgive you for that, then you can forgive me for the shit that I've done."

Brandon shook his head, and began to put on his clothes that were folded on the couch. He didn't understand how she could make one plus two equal four. A nigga would not walk away from any woman who was giving up the pussy.

"So you don't want to make this work?" Sasha asked, her voice cracking as she tried to hold it together.

"No, I don't want to make it work, Sasha. This whole situation is a fucking mess, and the only thing that I want to do is take care of my kids. All three of them." Brandon made himself clear, putting his shoes on. Sasha was about to respond when Brandon's cell phone began to ring.

"Yeah, Amekia," Brandon said, looking at Sasha with a smirk on his face.

"Where are you? My mother called and said that she would return Aziyah to me if I had a sit-down with her," Amekia said with movement in her background.

"I stopped over at Sasha's but I will be there soon."

"She told me not to tell anyone, but you're her father and I need somebody to be around for just in case."

"Okay, I got you, babe. I will be there just ready when I do." Brandon put some pep in his step.

"So you just going to fuck me and go running back to her like she's the wife and I'm the side chick!" Sasha fussed with her hand on her hips.

Brandon moved closer to Sasha, causing her to move back. He said, "My child is fucking missing and you want to stand there and worry about a fucking marriage that was doomed from the gate. You forget that your entitled ass daddy basically forced me to marry you so that he could get closer to my family and their church. I didn't want to be married, but your father and my parents thought it would be a good idea when they found out you were pregnant. I gotta go now, but I will be back to get my girls so they can meet their sister."

Sasha's mouth hung open, as she took in everything Brandon just said. It was the truth, but they hadn't spoken that truth in years. She figured that they had gotten over that hump and he actually loved her. Sasha had stood there for so long that she didn't realize that Brandon had walked out of her house, giving his daughters kisses on their forehead with promises of coming to get them for the weekend. She had gotten the girls situated in their room, before she went to her own room and cried her eyes out. She had to face the fact their marriage was over.

Chapter Five

While Brandon drove to Amekia's house, he couldn't help but think about the conversation he had with Sasha. He had to admit to himself that he had said some things to Sasha that he shouldn't have said, but they needed to be said. He was just making sure that she understood what he was saying. Reaching that far into the past was low of him, and he admitted that to himself, but it needed to be done. Brandon had enough time to ponder over his situation, and he'd concluded that Amekia was who he wanted to be with. He'd been lying to himself about his true feelings about Amekia. He knew he loved her but, for the last few months, he's been feeling things that he'd never felt for Sasha. Brandon thought back to the day he was forced to marry Sasha.

It was seven years ago, and at that time he was already with Sasha for three years. She was completing her last year in law school, and preparing to take the bar exam. Brandon was working for a construction company at the time, and was close to becoming a part of the management team. Brandon was high off of life as he made his way home. He was living with his parents still, but soon enough he would be in his own place because his parents were driving him crazy.

When he pulled up to his parents' house, he noticed that Sasha's father's car was in the driveway. Mr. Earl was a thorn in his side. He was always around his parents, sucking up, wanting to become a deacon at the church. Brandon's parents weren't trying to have another deacon at the church. So, when Mr. Earl would bring it up, they would change the subject. Mr. Earl never got the message, though.

Brandon exhaled as he got out of his car, and walked into his parents' house. No one was in the living room as he suspected, but he heard slightly raised voices coming from the kitchen, and that caused him to head in that direction. All conversation ceased when he got to the kitchen, and he noticed his parents, Mr. Earl, and Sasha's eyes. They were sitting at the table. Sasha's eyes were bloodshot, and he could tell that she had been crying.

"Umm, what's going?" Brandon asked, looking at everybody.

The look on his father's face showed he was beyond upset. That wasn't a look Brandon saw often, but when he did see it, he knew that whoever he was pissed at was going to be destroyed with his words. Sasha looked up at Brandon like she wanted to say something, but remained quiet.

"Congratulations, you are about to be a father." Mr. Earl spoke with a smirk on his face.

"What?" Brandon screeched as he looked down at Sasha.

"And Earl here is insisting that you marry his daughter," Brandon's mother spoke. For the first time, he realized that his mother had been crying as well.

"What?" Brandon screeched again.

He couldn't believe what the hell he had walked into. All he wanted to do was, walk the fuck back out of the room. He wasn't ready to be a parent. He had a great thing with Sasha, but to say that he was going to get married was never in the plans. He enjoyed his relationship with Sasha, and he knew for a fact that she was on birth control, so how did she end up pregnant!

"Brandon I—" Sasha began.

"How are you pregnant if you were on birth control? I saw you take them every day," Brandon stated.

"Young man, my daughter will not have a baby out of wedlock. You will make an honest woman out of her and marry her." Mr. Earl spoke matter-of-factly.

"How do you just expect me to marry her because she's pregnant? We are not ready for marriage nor a child."

"Brandon, abortion isn't an option. We don't believe in that," Brandon's mother spoke. Brandon looked on in disbelief because he was being thrown into a situation that he had no say-so. He knew that Mr. Earl was only suggesting such a thing because he thought it would help him with becoming a deacon. Brandon knew for sure that this wouldn't work at all. Brandon watched as his father walked over to his alcohol cabinet and poured himself a half glass of Jim Beam Bourbon. He sipped from the glass, and then placed the glass onto the counter.

Brandon's father began, "As much as I want to protest what Earl is suggesting, though he isn't saying anything that we don't know, you will go down to the courthouse Monday morning and apply for a marriage license and get married. That weekend we will have a small ceremony at the church." Brandon knew that when his father spoke, he was dead serious. Brandon couldn't help but drop his mouth open. He was being thrust into something that he didn't want to do. Brandon looked at Mr. Earl who stood there with a smile displayed on his face. Anger boiled inside of Brandon. He couldn't see himself being disrespectful to his parents, but Mr. Earl wasn't exempt from it. Brandon turned to Mr. Earl and displayed a smile on his own face.

"Mr. Earl, I don't know why you are standing there skinning and grinning. Just because I am marrying your daughter and giving you a grandchild, does not mean you will become a deacon at my parents' church. Sasha, I will talk to you later." After he'd spoken, Brandon turned

around. He heard his father chuckle as he made his way to his bedroom. Brandon was livid.

***

The knock on his car window brought Brandon back to reality, and he noticed that he had pulled up to Amekia's house and parked. Amekia stood next to the passenger side, dressed in sweats, a t-shirt, boots, and a scarf wrapped on her head. She looked like she was ready to stomp on her mother. Brandon unlocked the door, and Amekia got in.

"You've been out here for almost five minutes staring off into space, you good?" Amekia asked, as she put her seatbelt on.

"Oh yeah, I'm good. I barely got any sleep last night. Where are we headed?"

"She wants me to meet her in Buffalo Harbor State Park in Buffalo."

"What the fuck? That's like four hours away. What the fuck is she doing in Buffalo?" Brandon wondered.

"Years ago, when I was still a little girl, we lived near the harbor. The park wasn't built then, but she would always take me to sit near the water."

Brandon placed the address in the GPS, and followed the directions. On the ride to Buffalo, Brandon did everything in his power to try to occupy Amekia just to give her a little bit of normalcy. They talked about everything under the sun, and he even managed to make her laugh. When they were an hour away, Amekia decided to tell Brandon about the shit she had endured at the hands of her mother.

"And all she wants to do is, have a conversation with you and she will give us our daughter back?" Brandon asked.

"Yes, that's what she said."

"You're not dressed to have a conversation. You know like all hell you leaving that park after you whipped your mother's ass."

"I'm going to get our baby and then beat her ass. So when we get there, you're going to grab Aziyah and bring her back to the car and wait for me."

Brandon simply nodded and took her hand into his. After a few moments, Brandon said, "When we get back to Schenectady tonight, we need to talk about some things."

"Is it about anything that's bad 'cause I don't think I can deal with that."

Brandon let out a low chuckle and said, "No, it's not bad. At least I don't think so. But let's not worry about that right now. Let's go get our baby."

For the remainder of the ride they were quiet. Just the sounds from the radio engulfed the car. When they pulled up to the park, they looked around to check and see if anything was out of the ordinary. All they noticed were a few kids playing on the jungle gym, and their parents sitting on the benches watching their children.

"You ready?" Brandon asked before they climbed out of the car.

"Hell yeah."

"Where did she say she wanted to meet you?"

"By the water. She said there will be a wall of rocks and she will be along there."

"Okay, let's go."

Brandon and Amekia climbed out of the car and walked into the park and in the direction of the rock wall. They watched their surroundings, all the while making small talk. Amekia was the one who noticed her mother first. Mrs. Lewis sat on a large rock while a stroller sat in front of her.

Brandon and Amekia walked up to where Mrs. Lewis sat, with mean mugs on their faces.

"I asked you not to bring anyone," Mrs. Lewis said as she stood, pulling her shades from her face. Brandon looked between each woman, and was stunned silent at how much they resembled each other. As if they were twins instead of mother and daughter.

"This is her father. You better be lucky that I brought him and not the FBI like I wanted to."

Brandon walked closer to the stroller that Aziyah was in, and he saw that she was sleeping soundly. He held onto the handle of the stroller, and began to turn around, but Mrs. Lewis' voice stopped him.

"You are going to make a wonderful single father. Amekia is coming with me and will be married soon. She will no longer communicate with you or that bastard grand-child of mine."

"What?" Both Brandon and Amekia asked in shock.

"Brandon, take Aziyah to the car because she doesn't need to see her poor excuse of a grandmother getting her ass beat."

Brandon looked at Amekia and began to walk away. He paused in his steps, placed his hand on Amekia's waist and kissed her lips. Brandon made his way to put his daughter in the car afterwards.

"Do you suffer from mental illness? Why would you take my daughter and then think that I would willingly go with you anywhere?" Amekia asked with her lips tooted up in disgust.

Mrs. Lewis took a seat back onto one of the rocks, and placed her shades back over her eyes. She made it seem like she hadn't had a care in the world. She looked out over the harbor and continued to stay quiet.

"When I was a little girl, I was the apple of my father's eyes. There was nothing that I couldn't get away with. But my mother, that lady, was mean and hated my guts. When I was fourteen, my daddy passed away from a heart attack and, if you ask me, I think my mama had something to do with it. When my daddy passed, it was the worst. He was there to protect me from that woman's wrath but with him gone, it seemed like things got worse.

"My mother began to drink. It started with a few glasses of wine after dinner and then escalated to all-day drinking. At this time, my daddy had been gone for almost a year and things had gotten bad. My mother wasn't working, and my older brother had left home because he couldn't take my mother's bullshit anymore. My mother's drinking went on for a few more months until she had a horrible accident. She was drunker than she had ever been before, then she took a tumble down the stairs of our house. She'd broken her arm and leg and bruised a few ribs. She got her life together right after that, started to attend church, got a job, and for me it seemed like things were going to get better."

Mrs. Lewis took a moment to swipe away her tears. She'd never spoken about her life before her children's father came into her life, nor to any one besides him. Amekia didn't care for the story her mother was babbling about, but Amekia needed to prolong the reunion. Amekia's attention was brought back to reality when she had heard her mother's voice again.

"I was sixteen when my mother and I went to church one night. It wasn't unusual because we would always attend church at night for bible study. We arrived at the church, and I noticed that the usual bible study group wasn't there. However, Deacon Brown was there. I didn't like Deacon Brown because he would look at me funny. When Deacon

Brown heard us approaching, he turned towards us with a smile on his face. He had a thick brown envelope in his hands, and he handed it to my mother. She turned to me and told me to go with him. I wanted to question her, but we were in the house of the Lord and she told me that in the bible it said to honor thy mother and father, and she drilled into my head that if I didn't do just that, then I would be condemned to hell. And I believed her.

"Anyway, I went with Deacon Brown. We went to the basement of the church, where there was a table set up with two place settings and two glasses. There was a cot off to the darkest corners of the basement. My gut was telling me that something wasn't right, and that I needed to run out of there. I lost my chance when Deacon Brown locked the door behind us, using a key, then I started crying. Deacon Brown tried to soothe me by trying to get me to eat but I refused.

"Things took a turn for the worse when he got tired of hearing me cry and back-handed me out of my seat. I flew out of the chair as if I only weighed ten pounds. As he took his seat, he instructed me to take my clothes off and lay on the cot. When I didn't move fast enough, he threatened to hit me again. From that day up until I was eighteen, I was forced to marry Deacon Brown. No one in the church knew what my mother and Deacon Brown had done, and everyone was surprised when we had gotten married. Of course, there were whispers around the church but no one ever had the gall to say anything.

"Fast forward six years after we wed, Deacon Brown started to show interest in other girls in the church. We argued about it often. Not because he wasn't interested in me anymore but just to fuck on another little girl. I figured I could save her. That was until he wouldn't stop bothering her. He constantly said degrading things to her and was always trying to touch her. She, unlike me, spoke up and told her father and he killed my husband. Two years later, I found your father."

Amekia stood there with no expression on her face. She didn't understand why her mother felt the need to tell her the story. She guessed that her mother felt remorseful for what she did to her. But then again, Amekia could care less.

"I'm ready to bring you home. Allow that man to take that child you both have created. I want you to meet Nigel. I told him all about you, and he can't wait to marry you and give me some grandbabies." Mrs. Lewis had a wide smile on her face.

Amekia placed her hands on her hips, squinted, and tucked her bottom lip into her mouth. Her blood boiled as she brought her hand back to the pits of hell and smacked flames out of her mother. She smacked her mother so hard from off of the rock that she spun twice before she landed on the ground.

"It must be crack that you smoking for you to think I would go anywhere with your sick demented ass! You think that I'm that little girl that you had trapped in your home years ago!" Amekia yelled. Children and their parents that were on the playground stopped what they were doing to watch the show that Amekia was giving. She was standing over her mother; one hand was full of hair, and the other was smashing into her face.

"Hey! That's enough!" Amekia heard a gruff voice yell. Next thing Amekia knew, she was lifted off of her mother, and a team of FBI agents swarmed her mother. Mrs. Lewis was a bloody mess, as she was picked up from the ground and handcuffed. One of the agents escorted Amekia to the car where Brandon was looking on with Aziyah in his arms.

"Miss Franklin," the agent began, "I am going to let you off of the hook with what you have done due to the circumstances. We advise that you go straight to Schenectady and have your daughter looked at by a doctor just to be on the safe side." The agent watched Amekia take Aziyah out of Brandon's arms and smother her with kisses.

"Thank you," Brandon simply stated and shook the agent's hand. Brandon took Aziyah from Amekia, and placed her in the car seat. Amekia got inside the car and let out fresh tears from her face. She was relieved that her daughter was back in her care. From what she could see, Aziyah was healthy. Brandon joined Amekia when he was done putting Aziyah in her seat. When he noticed that Amekia was crying, he took her into his arms and rubbed her back. Her shoulders shook with each sob as she cried with relief.

"Shh. It's okay now, Amekia. We got our baby girl back, and we could move on from this."

Amekia wiped tears from her face. "She needs to be locked up in a mental institution. Jail isn't going to work. She needs close monitoring and medication."

"You are going to have to testify in court, so make that your main argument."

"I know. Thank you, Brandon."

Brandon grabbed Amekia's hand, and placed a kiss on the back of it. He responded, "No need to thank me. She's my child too, and I'm going to go to the ends of the earth behind her and her sisters."

"Speaking of, I think it's time that Alexis and Aliana met their sister."

Brandon stole a quick glance at Amekia to silently ask her if she was sure. He wanted nothing more for Alexis and Aliana to meet Aziyah, but he didn't want the drama from

Amekia nor Sasha. Amekia nodded, letting Brandon know that she was serious. With a nod he began to think about his daughters meeting their new sibling. On the way home, Amekia made a quick call to Jade to let her know that she had gotten Aziyah back. Jade gave Amekia a quick update on Carmen, and Amekia promised that as soon as she could, she would go visit Carmen. A few moments later, Amekia hung up and sat back in her seat. She was finally able to breathe and work on getting her life back on track.

Chapter Six

Jade sat in front of her full body mirror on the floor, concentrating on putting on her mink lashes. It had been so long since she had done a full face of make-up that she feared she would look like a clown. Jade had been getting individual lashes for the past few years, but her date with Timothy had just been a few hours away, so she didn't have time to get her usual set. Her lash lady was always booked, so to do a walk in on a Friday would have cut it real close. She settled on applying the lashes herself instead of going out looking like a bald baby eagle.

After ten minutes of trying to put her lashes on, she finally got it and headed to her closet to find something to wear. Timothy told her that where they were going was going to be a surprise, but to dress down. He'd added that she didn't need to be too dressy. He was picking her up at eight-thirty and around that time, the sun would start to go down. September was just a week away, and the weather was going to change. Jade decided to rock black ripped jeans, a white shirt with a flower etched in black. On her feet she threw on classic black and white chucks. Jade combed her hair down from the wrap she had it in, threw in her oversized hoop earrings, and was satisfied with her look.

Ding! Ding!

Jade's phone notified her that she had a text message. She knew that it wasn't time for Timothy to come pick her up, so she had no clue it was hitting her up. Looking at her phone, her eyebrows raised, not recognizing the number but was surprised by the content of the text.

(518)-555-2363: Jade this is Denise. I know that you may be shocked from hearing me but it seems like you're one out of all of Carmen's friends to have the most common sense. It

seems like Sasha is dead set on blaming me for the horrible accident that Carmen was in. Please give me a call so that I can clear my name.

Jade sucked her teeth when she was done reading the text because she felt the same way as Sasha. Sasha was just a natural beast and overprotective. After all, she was a damn good lawyer trained to sniff out bullshit as if she was a bloodhound. Sasha knew that if Denise didn't start the fire herself, she knew that Denise knew who did, and Jade was going to go through hell or high-water in order to put the pieces all together.

Jade didn't respond right away because she had to finish getting ready for her date. Then she had an idea. Picking up her phone, she sent a text to Sasha, letting her know that in a few days she was going to need her help. With a satisfied smirk, Jade walked to her kitchen, pulled her bottle of strawberry *Barefoot* wine, and poured some in a wine goblet. Her nerves were starting to get the best of her. The last time she was on a date, it was with Darion before the HIV debacle. Timothy showed a significant amount of interest in her, but he could always change his mind. She turned her head to look at the time on the microwave, and realized that it was eight-thirty-five.

"Shit!" she exclaimed out loud, as she threw back the last of her wine and popped a piece of gum in her mouth before heading to the door. She opened the door with a smile plastered on her face.

"Hey," Timothy said, returning the same nervous smile that Jade was displaying.

"Hey. Sorry it took so long to get to the door. I was lost in my thoughts about something."

"Are you ready?" Timothy asked.

"I am. Let me just grab my purse and phone, and we can be on our way. Are you going to tell me where we are going?"

Timothy chuckled and responded, "No. It's going to be a surprise until we get to where we are going. However, I will say that one of the places that we are going is to get something to eat. Do you want to go eat first?"

"Nah…I think I got a few more hours left in me to wait."

"Okay then. Go ahead and grab your things and we can go."

Jade nodded as she walked into her bedroom to grab her things. Before heading back to the door, she took a deep breath and headed back to him. Timothy stood on the porch, waiting for Jade. When she returned, she locked up her house and walked to his car, her arm looped through his at the elbow. Jade was impressed that he didn't only open the car door for her, but also waited until she was comfortable before closing the door. When he got in, he handed her a dozen yellow tulips. To say she was shocked by these gestures was an understatement. She simply thanked him with a smile on her face, and enjoyed the ride.

While they made their way to their destination, they talked about everything under the sun. Jade thought it was just a distraction to keep her from asking where they were going. While she enjoyed the conversation and thought Timothy was funny, she couldn't help but have an annoying feeling that he was taking her off to be slaughtered. Thirty minutes later, they arrived at a huge parking lot with several different businesses, and she couldn't pinpoint where they were going. She was relieved to know that she was going to be in a public place, and not in somebody's field being buried like other innocent victims.

"There are different places where we can go, which one are we going in?" Jade asked as she looked around.

"We are standing in front of it," Timothy said with a bright smile on his face. Jade turned around to face the direction that Timothy was facing. They were standing in front of a building that had the words *'Spare Time'* on the front.

"Bowling?" Jade asked, confused. She was okay with bowling, but wondered why he wanted to keep it a secret.

"Oh, no, ma'am. That's just the main thing here. Let's go inside so that we can begin."

Timothy thought he was so funny by keeping a secret from Jade. He knew that she would enjoy the surprise and it would earn him brownie points. As they entered, a woman greeted them, calling Timothy by name, and made small talk. They followed the woman shortly after, passed the bowling alley, and to a separate room. The woman gave Timothy a hug and went on her merry way. Jade gave Timothy a side eye, and he chuckled at the look.

"Now, come here so that I can put this blindfold over your eyes," Timothy stated, causing Jade to cast a sideways glance towards him. Reluctantly, she turned her back towards him and allowed him to place the blindfold over her eyes. She felt Timothy grab her hand, and she followed him. They entered through a door, and some laughter went off in the distance. Jade felt Timothy put something over her head that rested on her chest. *What the fuck is going on?* she thought.

"Okay, I am going to take the blindfold off of you. You ready?" Timothy asked. Jade was eager as fuck to have the blindfold off her face. Once it was off her face, she blinked several times as her eyes adjusted to the neon lights before her. There was a maze of neon lights in front of her, and she watched people run around with vests on and laser guns pointed at each other. Jade's eyes lit up. She remembered instantly one night she had told him that she had always wanted to go on fun dates such as laser tag, and she was excited that he was listening.

"Oh my God!" Jade exclaimed, and turned her attention to Timothy. He had a wide smile on his face.

"That woman was my cousin, she works here and gave us a discount on whatever we're gonna do here today. You ready?"

"Man, hell yeah. Where can I put my purse?"

"Let me get it so that I could give it to my cousin and she could lock it up."

Jade handed him her purse, and he disappeared through the door. Jade couldn't help but continue to smile. She liked that he not only listened to her but also heard her. There had been so many times that she would date somebody and have them listen, but it was hard for them to hear her. So often she would feel like she wasn't being heard, and a man who seemed like he dropped from out of the sky did something that several men couldn't.

Moments later, Timothy came back inside with a big smile on his face. They walked over to the counter, where they were handed laser guns and vests. With excitement radiating through her body, Jade shot Timothy in the chest and ran away. They went back and forth, shooting each other and having a good time. An hour later, they left the laser tag room and went to the main area, where they got food. She settled on loaded nachos, and Timothy had a double cheeseburger and fries. Finding a seat was easy because *Spare Time* was closing soon.

"Thank you so much. I had the time of my life tonight." Jade spoke while sipping her soda through a straw.

"You don't have to thank me. I'm just trying to make sure that you keep a smile on your face. That shit looks damn good on you."

"I'm flattered."

"Really and truly, Jade, you look damn good and captivating," Timothy said with a cute smile.

Jade's mouth dropped open, as she tried to shield her eyes out of the slight embarrassment that she felt. Their laughter was cut short when a woman walked up to their table unannounced. Timothy noticed first and spoke.

"Can we help you?" he asked, causing Jade to look up from her nachos. She took one look at the woman, and heat radiated through her body.

"You can't but she can," the woman said.

Jade sucked her teeth and said, "Tanya, what the fuck you want?"

"I got a call from Darion today. You know where he called me from?" Tanya said with an evil expression on her face.

"Actually, I do. And I'm pretty sure it's from jail."

"Of course you know, 'cause you're the trifling bitch that put him there."

Jade chuckled and rubbed her hands on a napkin. Sauce from the nachos was on them. Jade scooted her chair back, just in case she had to stand up. She replied. "He is the trifling one in this situation, Tanya. Again, what do you want? If that's what you wanted, then you can go about your business."

"You need to drop whatever charges you have against him. He didn't tell me, but I'm sure that they are just as bogus as that cheap ass wig that you got on top of your head."

Tanya smirked, thinking that she had one up on Jade. What Tanya didn't know was that it took more than a weak ass wig joke to cause Jade to come off her rocker. Jade shook her head because it would take a bum ass nigga to not tell his so-called girlfriend what he did. Probably wasn't even his first time doing that shit, and it caused Jade to shudder.

"That man is in there for attempting to rape me in front of my house, in broad daylight—He deserves to be in there," Jade explained. Not that she had to, but she needed to set Tanya straight.

"You're lying! He didn't try to rape you! That's probably something you made up for this nigga! Darion is not a rapist, you lying ass hoe!" Tanya yelled, drawing attention to where they were sitting.

Timothy looked at Tanya with disgust, as he decided that he had heard enough. He shook his head as he stood up and said, "Come on, Jade. You don't even have to put up with this shit."

Jade stood up while grabbing her purse. She was going to walk away and not say anything else to Tanya, but there was a gnawing feeling that wouldn't allow her to keep walking. She stopped in front of Tanya and said, "I don't know what's up with women who choose not to believe another woman when she says a man has tried to or has raped her. It is women like you in this society of doubting Thomases that are so quick to condemn a woman for speaking out against the monster that raped her. Then wonder why it takes women years to summon up the courage to speak. Tanya, I don't have to explain shit to you. I just pray that you find out what a real monster that man is."

Jade walked away, leaving Tanya stuck in her place with her mouth hanging open. Jade was trying everything in her body to not bust out in tears. This was her first real date in a long time, and it had been ruined. Before Jade reached the exit, she felt a tug on her hair that ripped through her scalp. Before she knew it, her back landed against the floor. In a flash, Tanya was on top of her, punching her in the face. Tanya got a few licks in before Timothy picked her up off of Jade, and Jade immediately jumped up with fire burning in her. She moved around Timothy and attacked Tanya, delivering body blows that caused Tanya to fold like a chair.

"Bitch, you crazy? I owe you an ass whooping from you smashing in my damn window! You thought I forgot about that?" Jade yelled, as she sat on top of Tanya and rained blows on her face. Timothy picked Jade's tiny frame up, and carried her outside with ease. Jade left Tanya bloody on the floor still talking shit. A crowd had formed to make sure that Tanya was okay. Once she had gotten up, she followed behind Timothy and Jade out to the parking lot, spewing hate.

"I hope you ain't fuck her yet because she out here with a death sentence on that stank ass pussy! She got death between her legs, nigga, you better strap up before you fuck her!" Tanya yelled for everyone to hear. Fire built up inside of Jade that she had never felt before. She was in full attack mode until Timothy stood in front of Jade, and made her look at him. Tanya continued to make a scene and yell. Timothy saw the hurt in Jade's eyes. It hurt him to his soul to see her that hurt. Timothy took Jade by the hand, led her back to his car, and helped her inside. Jade could no longer hold her tears in. Timothy climbed in just as Jade was screaming at the top of her lungs and punching his dashboard. There was nothing that Timothy could have done to make Jade feel better, so he allowed her to get her frustrations out.

"It's going to be okay," Timothy said while rubbing Jade's back.

"No, it's not, Timothy! I have a disease that I can't get rid of! This shit will never be okay! I won't ever forget that I am HIV positive because there are bitches like Tanya who will always throw that shit in my face!" Jade cried. She was hurt beyond measure. The way Tanya put her business on blast had her wanting to murder her. She had never been so disrespected like that, and Jade vowed to herself that she would make sure that Tanya would get hers.

"Jade, don't let what that woman said to you get you down. She's hurting over something that you have no control over and when hurt people are hurt, they tend to want to hurt others. You can't allow that shit to get to you." In Jade's mind, she knew the words that Timothy was saying were true, but she wasn't in her right frame of mind and wasn't thinking clearly.

"Nah, fuck all that, Timothy! Since I stopped fucking with that nigga, she has been a thorn in my side. She broke my living room window just because she found out that he was cheating on her. I'm past the bullshit about hurt people hurting people. She did that out of spite and if I was a ruthless bitch and held a weapon on me, she would have been more than hurt, and I would have been on my way to jail. Timothy, please just take me home." Jade sniffled. She tried wiping her tears away, but they wouldn't stop falling. Timothy simply dropped the situation, placed his car in drive, and drove off. During the whole ride back to Schenectady, Jade held her face in her hands and cried. Timothy hadn't known Jade that long, but his heart went out to her. He wished that there could be something that he could do to make her feel better.

Half an hour later, Jade felt the car stop. She opened her eyes. They felt puffy, and she just knew that they were bloodshot. She looked out of the window, and noticed that she wasn't in front of her house.

"Where are we?" Jade asked, sounding as if she had a cold.

"We are in front of my house," Timothy said, as he turned the car off and turned towards Jade.

Jade sighed and said, "Today was nice up until that shit with Tanya, and I appreciate what you've done. But right now I just want to go home."

Timothy took his time before he answered Jade. He said, "I can't say that I know how you feel because I don't. But I will say that I won't allow what happened with Tanya to take any more energy off you. We're gonna go in and enjoy a movie and then I can take you home. Is that cool with you?"

Jade wanted to protest, but she felt like part of the night ending the way it did was her fault. The least she could do would be to take him up on his offer. She looked at Timothy and smiled as best as she could. She said, "Okay. I'm cool with that."

Timothy grinned and climbed out of the car. He went over to Jade's side of the car, and helped her out of the car. Timothy had parked his car in his driveway and for the first time, Jade noticed how massive his house was. The exterior of the house was made of red bricks, and the windows were white trimmed with black shutters. Timothy grabbed Jade's hand, and led her up to his door. The door was made of solid wood, and had a window in the middle.

Timothy unlocked the door, and entered into a long hallway. Timothy turned to the wall to turn his alarm system off, while Jade took in the extravagant home that was before her. To her right there was a living room with marble walls, and everything was decorated in white and silver. To her left, there was another living room, and this one was decorated in black, deep mahogany brown, and smoky grey.

Timothy looked at Jade. “You can have a seat in the living room,” he said. “Make yourself comfortable while I go make us something to drink,” he added, then walked away too fast, and Jade couldn’t ask him which living room he wanted her to go into. For a few seconds she looked between the two living rooms, and finally decided to go into the darker colored living room.

The couch she sat on seemed to be made out of the softest butter leather that she had ever felt. Her body sunk right in, and she felt like she was in heaven. In front of her was a glass coffee table. There was a small pile of magazines and about four remote controls sitting on top. She looked around, but didn’t see a TV. Her mother taught her when she was younger: *As company, never touch nothing, whether the owner of the house gave you the green light or not.* So she just sat back in silence on the couch. She didn’t really know how tired she was, or notice that Timothy was taking a little too long to come back with their drinks. She allowed her eyes to close. Before long, she was asleep.

Timothy walked into the living room with their drinks of champagne in flutes, and noticed Jade was lying comfortably on the couch with her head on the arm rest. He placed the flutes on the coffee table, and squatted down. He pushed the hair from her face, admiring her beauty. She looked so peaceful sleeping that he didn’t want to wake her up. But he had a surprise for her.

“Jade, I know you are comfortable but I got a surprise for you,” Timothy said, as he softly shook her from her slumber.

"Huh? Where the hell am I?" Jade asked, sitting up on the couch in alarm. Her head was on a swivel until her eyes met Timothy's, and that's when she knew where she was.

Timothy couldn't help himself, and he laughed. He said, "I hope you don't wake up like that every day."

Jade scrunched up her face and playfully swatted his arm. She said, "You play too much, that wasn't even funny."

"If you saw your face how I saw it, you would be laughing too," Timothy said, and continued to laugh.

Jade stretched and reached for one of the flutes, and took a short sip of the expensive bubbly. Timothy followed suit and took a sip of his drink. Climbing up from the floor where he sat, he got up, grabbing her hand. Jade looked at him, and placed her flute back on the table. His eyes told her to follow him, and she did. They went down the long hallway, making a right at the end. They approached a door that was closed, but Timothy quickly changed that. They entered a huge bathroom. There was a shower that expanded from one wall to the other wall. There was a bench in the middle of the shower, and three shower heads were placed on the three walls. The glass that was the shower door was so crystal clear it looked like the door was never touched. The lights were dimmed down, and candles placed around the bathroom. In the middle of the bathroom floor sat a white porcelain claw foot tub filled with hot water and bubbles. Red rose petals laid out on top of the bubbles.

"You had a long day, well, a rough past two hours and I figured that I could do something to help you relax. The water has some lavender and eucalyptus bath salts, and the bubbles are the same. I know you don't have extra clothes here but I got some basketball shorts and a tee shirt you can rock while your clothes are washing and drying."

Jade was rendered silent as she watched Timothy turn and walk out of the bathroom, and decided to take him up on his offer. She began to strip out of her clothes, and folded them to place them on the toilet. Taking one last look around the bathroom, she climbed into the bathtub. The hot water immediately relaxed her, as her body sank deeper and deeper into the tub.

Jade leaned her head against the tub and closed her eyes. All of the tension she was holding in left her body. The bathroom door opened, and she heard Timothy come in. He informed her that he was going to grab her clothes and would check back with her in twenty minutes. She managed a grunt to acknowledge that she heard him.

Twenty minutes later: Jade was just wrapping a plush white towel over her body after she stepped out of the shower. Jade had stayed in the shower for ten minutes after Timothy had left only to jump in the shower after locating his towels. Timothy knocked on the door, and came in eyeing Jade sitting on the tub.

"I left a new, fresh pair of boxer briefs straight from the pack on the bed with gym shorts and a tee—I'll be in the living room waiting to watch a movie," Timothy said.

With laughter in her voice, Jane said: "I'll be there. Thank you, now get out."

Timothy shook his head as he exited the bathroom. Jade exited moments after Timothy did, and found the master bedroom. The room was massive. A California king-sized bed was against the wall that faced the doorway. The headboard and platform was made out of velvet material. Emerald green and black pillows adorned the bed, which was covered in black silk sheets. There was a nightstand on either side of the bed, and crystal lamps sat on each night table. A full-length square mirror hung from the wall to the left in between the two floor-to-ceiling windows. Jade spotted the clothes folded neatly on the bed, and quickly put them on. Although she was impressed with what she saw, she didn't want to have Timothy thinking that she was snooping. Jade decided on just wearing the briefs and T-shirt, leaving the shorts on the bed. Grabbing the towel from the floor, she held it draped across her arm and made her way to the living room.

"Where would you like for me to put this towel?" Jade asked once she was inside the living room.

"Let me show you to the laundry room," Timothy told her and walked towards the kitchen. The laundry room was the size of a small walk-in closet with top-of-the-line washer and dryer. She made a mental note to ask him what he did for a living.

"What movie are we watching?" Jade asked, as they took a seat on the couch.

"I hope you like action because I've been trying to watch the new Godzilla movie that just came out," Timothy said as he pressed *play* on the DVD player.

"Oh my God! Me too. You got popcorn?"

Timothy chuckled at her excitement. He said, "Yeah, let me go get that."

Timothy dipped off to the kitchen to put some popcorn in the microwave. When he came back, they got comfortable and watched the movie. Forty-five minutes later, Jade had a pillow under her head that balanced on Timothy's lap. Her mouth was wide open, and she was visiting dreamland. Timothy sat up against the couch with his head tucked into his chest. Both of them enjoyed the sleep that they so desperately needed.

Chapter Seven

Sasha sat in her car at her mother-in-law's house after a long day of work. She just wanted to go home, soak in a hot bubble bath, and go to sleep butt-naked afterward. Sasha knew that it would never happen. Brandon's mother, Betty, had her girls for the summer during the day, while Sasha had them at night. That was coming to an end because school was back in session the next day, and Sasha was grateful that she wouldn't have to see her mother-in-law's face. Sasha sat in her car, and thought about how she went from married with minimal help to being a single parent with no help, in just a blink of an eye. When she came back to reality, she climbed out of the car, and walked sluggishly to the house.

Sasha rang the doorbell and waited for either Betty or Robert to open the door. She could hear her girls laughing through the door, and it put a smile on her face. The locks turning caused Sasha to stand up straight, smooth her clothes, and plaster a fake smile on her face. Betty stood on the opposite end of the door, and looked Sasha up and down in disgust. Betty was still under the impression that Sasha was still getting a divorce. Betty didn't know Sasha had recanted on that and attempted to work on her marriage. Or so Sasha thought. She knew that Brandon didn't say anything because Betty didn't mention it. Betty was the type to throw shit in your face just to let you know that she knew.

"The girls are in the den with their father," Betty said with a sneaky smirk on her face. Sasha eyed Betty as she made her way inside the house and moved towards the den. As she got closer to the den, she heard her daughters squealing with excitement in their voices. Wondering why they were so excited, she sped her pace up. She stopped in her tracks when she got to the doorway. Her heartbeat thumped against her chest like it was an African drum. Brandon and their daughters were sitting on the floor swooning over something. When she walked in, she noticed that in front of them was an almost four-month-old Aziyah inside of a swing, bright eyed, and with a smile on her face. Sasha wasn't ready for this, and it smacked her in the face.

"Mommy!" Aliana yelled when she noticed her mother in the room. That shook Sasha out of her stupor, and she placed a smile on her face.

"Hi, my babies," she said, as she reached her arms out for them to come hug her.

"What up, Sasha?" Brandon asked, not turning to her.

"Hey, Brandon."

"Mama, can we stay? I want to play with my baby sister." Alexis asked while looking up at her mother.

"Oh, no, honey. I'm sorry. First day of school is tomorrow. But you can on the weekend."

"Aww, man, I hate school." Aliana pouted.

Brandon eyed his daughter. "Aye, don't let me ever hear you say that again. There will be plenty of time for you to play with your sister. Always remember that school is important."

"Yes, Daddy," Aliana said with her lips pouted. Her eyes began to look watery, like she was about to cry, but one look from her father dried that shit right away.

"Okay, girls, go get your things so that we can go home and get ready for school," Sasha said with yet another fake smile on her face. Aliana and Alex ran out of the room to go gather their things. Sasha looked at Brandon as he wiggled a rattle in front of her face.

"I never thought that we would be here," Sasha said, as she folded her arms across her chest and leaned against the door frame.

"Sasha, it was bound to happen. Once Aliana started going to school and you went back to work, things changed. Our marriage was doomed to begin with, if you want to be honest. Just because we were having a child together didn't mean that we had to get married. We allowed our parents to meddle in our relationship and for the first two years, that's all they did. More so your pops than my parents."

"Tut-tut! Playboy! Don't blame my daddy. Especially because he is in a grave and not here to defend himself!" Sasha yelled, and Aziyah began to cry. Brandon looked behind him at Sasha who wore a I-don't-give-a-fuck look on her face. Brandon shook his head and reached inside of the swing to settle Aziyah.

"I know, Zi-Zi, that mean old lady made you cry. Daddy sorry." Brandon cooed in Aziyah's ear as he rocked her back and forth.

"This is pointless. Let me go before some shit gets said that doesn't need to be said." Sasha hissed while waving her hand at her side.

"Nah, if you got something to say, say that shit. You grown, right? Because you were damn grown when you cheated on me with a convicted felon, who by the way was using you to get him off to justify him murdering two people! One of whom is a woman at that!" Brandon shouted.

"You acting like I was the one who cheated first! You know what? I'm going to exit left." Sasha wanted to cry. She was furious. To her, she felt like everybody thought she was in the wrong. Sasha had suspicions of Brandon cheating, but never had the proof. She stayed with him then when she should have left in order to avoid this drama. Before Sasha allowed her tears to fall, she marched into the living room and told her daughters to come on. Alexis and Aliana solemnly walked over to their grandmother, and gave her a hug. She smirked at Sasha yet again. Sasha rolled her eyes at Betty, and joined her girls outside. She was helping her girls with their seat belts when she felt a presence behind her. She closed the car door, and turned around to a smug face Betty.

"How can I help you? You said bye to the girls already, so what do you want?" Sasha asked, becoming tired of this little game that Betty was playing.

"Oh no, I want to speak with you. And do you not have any respect for your elders? What have your parents taught you while they were here?" Betty spoke with malice in her voice, hoping she hit a soft spot in Sasha to bring her down a few notches.

"Listen, Betty, I have had nothing but the utmost respect for you, but you are pushing it. My parents are no longer here and you need not to speak on them. You and I don't need to speak on anything if it ain't got shit to do with my daughters." Sasha's tone was laced with equal malice. She moved to the driver side door when Betty presented her with a brown legal envelope.

"Brandon went to get divorce papers drawn and wanted me to give them to you," Betty simply stated after Sasha grabbed the envelope. With that same smirk she had on her face, Betty turned around and walked back to her house. Sasha watched as Betty closed the door behind. Sasha was angry. She felt played. Brandon wasn't man enough to give her the papers himself. Fire ripped through her body. Sasha climbed into her car and drove away from her in-laws' house. Fuck a hot bath and sleep; she needed a few shots to calm her nerves.

***

Carmen could hear the sounds of machines around her, as she willed herself to open her eyes. She didn't know how long she had been sleeping, but she needed to wake her ass up. She was thirsty and needed to pee so bad that it hurt. In Carmen's mind, she replayed the times that she heard her friends talking to her, and she remembered that she never heard Amekia's voice. Thinking about Amekia did just the right trick in order for her eyes to open. She blinked several times, as she looked up at the ceiling, slowly. She looked at the machines that were at the head of her bed. She heard sniffling, and her eyes looked in the direction of the noise. Amekia was sitting next to her bed, patting her eyes dry. Removing the tissue from her face, she looked at Carmen and paused when she realized that Carmen's eyes were open. Amekia was a little afraid because Carmen looked at her eyes wide and unblinking. They stared at each other until Carmen blinked and scared Amekia out of her seat. If Carmen could have laughed, she would have.

"Oh my God! I need a nurse in here! My friend is awake!" Amekia yelled, rushing to the door. Nurses and a doctor filed into the room, pushing Amekia out of the room. She called up Jade, crying and screaming into the phone, letting her know that Carmen was now awake. Ten minutes passed, and everyone filed out of Carmen's room. They had taken the tube from her mouth, and her bed was now in a sitting up position. Amekia crept into Carmen's room with a huge smile on her face.

"Why the fuck are you just now getting up here, heffa?" Carmen asked with a smile on her face.

With tears running down her cheeks, Amekia replied. "Oh, it was a bunch of shit that prevented me from coming over to see you. I wanted nothing more than to be by your side. I feel horrible." If her mother hadn't kidnapped her daughter, she would have been by Carmen's bedside.

"Oh, believe me, I know. Just because I wasn't here speaking with them other bitches, they talked me half to death, and I know what happened. I'm sorry that your mother did what she did, and I can't help but feel like I was a part of that. If we hadn't invited her to your welcome home party, then she wouldn't have even known that you had a baby." Fresh tears rolled down Carmen's cheeks.

"You didn't do anything wrong, Carmen, so please don't carry that burden. My mother has been a piece of shit my whole life. I should have known from the beginning that it was her, and I feel so bad that it never crossed my mind. If I did, I think I would have gotten Aziyah back sooner. Every time I look at my baby girl's face, I feel like a failure because I couldn't protect her." Sadness lined Amekia's features. She didn't mean to lay all of that on Carmen, but it had been eating her up and she had no one to vent to. Several times, she attempted to tell Brandon what happened. But then again, she would stop when she would think that he would judge her.

"Aww, Amekia, things are going to be okay. You just told me that I can't carry the burden of Aziyah having gone missing, and you can't hold onto you feeling like you didn't protect her." Carmen reached over and touched Amekia's hand.

"Look at me babbling about my fucking drama. I should be asking you if you are okay. What did the doctor say?"

"Well, they said that someone would be here in a few minutes, to take me to get CAT scans and MRI's. They want to check my brain function. They said that they are sure that everything is okay up there because I'm up and alert, speaking properly as well. They said that I should be fine."

"Do you know who would do this shit to you?" Amekia asked, wondering what everyone was thinking when the accident first happened.

"It was Denise. I didn't see her, though. Hell, I didn't see anyone, but I know it was her. We had gotten into a fight over me posting to her Facebook page blowing her up to her family. We were going at it. One minute, I was watching Love & Hip Hop, and I remember falling asleep. That's when I realized that I was in the hospital."

"I'm going to beat the fuck out of that bitch. Don't you know that she had the nerve to contact Jade and ask Jade to hear her out! That she had nothing to do with what happened to you."

Carmen shook her head in disbelief. Since she had left her old job, the one that drove her to almost kill herself, she hadn't had any beef with anybody. Her girls knew this, so it was right for them to accuse Denise of having something to do with it. Carmen said, "She may have not done the deed herself, but I know that she knows who did it."

Both Carmen and Amekia got quiet, their minds swimming with deep thoughts. Amekia wanted nothing more than to get revenge for Carmen. The poor woman had been laid up in the hospital for the past two months in a coma because somebody woke up one day and chose to set her house on fire. Amekia was livid. Rushed footsteps coming from behind Amekia brought her back to reality, and she turned to see who it was. Jade was rushing down the hallway, breathing heavily and carrying flowers.

"I got here as soon as I could—School is open again and I had to let my principal know this was an emergency," Jade said, trying to catch her breath while holding onto Amekia's arm.

"Well, hello to you too, bitch," Carmen said with a smile on her face. Jade ran over to the bed, and wrapped her arms around Carmen. As much as Carmen wanted to warn Jade that she was hurting her, it had been a while since Carmen felt someone's arms around her, and she accepted the pain she was temporarily in.

Jade pulled away, wiping away the tears that formed in her eyes. She asked, "What did the doctors say?"

"They said that they wanted to take me to do some tests just to check my brain function and things like that, but I feel fine. Besides the pain, I don't think that I would be able to tell myself that I was in an accident. I feel fine. They were surprised that once they got the tube out my mouth that I was speaking so clearly."

Jade smiled because it was good to have her friend back.

"Sasha didn't get here yet?" Jade asked.

"Nah," Amekia responded with a roll of her eyes.

Carmen sighed and asked, "Y'all still going at it?"

"I haven't spoken a word to that woman since the last fight we had. I don't have anything to say to her." Amekia pouted while folding her arms.

With a serious tone, Carmen addressed Amekia. "You do realize that you were in the wrong, right, Amekia? Now I don't agree with all that fighting shit because we are all grown and we are all friends, and I think that we should be able to talk to one another, but you do realize that you were the one who slept with and had a baby with her husband. She was your best friend. How could you do that?"

Amekia shook her head because now was not a good time for Carmen to try to come at her about Sasha. She lived with that fact every day; that she betrayed one of her best friends. She knew it was wrong, but she did it anyway. No one could ever ask her how she could do that when she was trying to figure that out herself.

"Look, I—" Amekia started, but Carmen interrupted her.

"Sasha sat next to my bed more than once crying her eyes out because of this situation. Sometimes she wanted her husband back, and other times she wanted her best friend back. She was angry, sad, and confused at how you and Brandon did what y'all did. You need to put your pride to the side and apologize to Sasha because she was more hurt with your betrayal than Brandon's. That woman is hurting and nobody knows because she puts a brave face on for everybody. Something needs to get fixed before Sasha reaches a breaking point that she cannot return from. And, Amekia, if you don't do it for anyone, do it for Aziyah. Because at the end of the day, Sasha's girls are her sisters and y'all gonna have to be around each other at some point, and I'll be damned if I'm breaking up any more fights between my friends."

The room was silent until Jade broke out in a round of applause. She snapped her fingers and said, "Yasss, fresh from a coma and getting these bitches together!"

Carmen and Amekia couldn't help but laugh. Carmen said, "Get your dumb ass out my room."

They spoke for a few more minutes until nurses came to get Carmen to run her tests. Both Amekia and Jade agreed to go to the hospital cafeteria to have lunch. Amekia was mostly quiet, and listened to Jade talk about this Timothy character that she had been seeing for a little while now. What Carmen had said to Amekia was hitting her hard, and she knew deep inside that Carmen was right. But Amekia was stubborn through and through, and would never admit that Carmen was right. At least not out loud.

Chapter Eight

Sasha was in court when she had received a missed call from Jade. When she was finally able to listen to voicemail, it was four o'clock, and she was just leaving the courthouse. She called Brandon and asked him if he could pick up the girls from their after-school program they were in, and explained that Carmen was up. On her way to the hospital, she hoped that at least Amekia was gone. There was no way in hell that she would be able to see her, considering how her day had been. The man that she was defending didn't want to cop to a plea because he said he was innocent. It was hard for her to defend that he was innocent when he was caught by an undercover cop selling him drugs. To top that, he was caught on surveillance plenty of times selling drugs. He was screaming in the courtroom, and they had to go to recess twice because of his outbreaks. The recesses took her all day in court.

As Sasha was walking off the elevator on the burn unit, she sighed and made her way to Carmen's room. Luckily for her, both Amekia and Jade weren't there. She was happy to speak with her friend in peace. When she entered the room, Carmen was laying with her eyes closed. Sasha walked over, and placed her hand over Carmen's, causing Carmen's eyes to pop open.

"Shit! Why would you open your eyes like that? Scared me shitless," Sasha said, and immediately wrapped Carmen in a hug.

"Bitch, I can't breathe," Carmen mumbled into Sasha's breast.

"Oh, shit! I'm sorry. I just missed hearing your voice, friend." Sasha laughed.

"Yeah, but you don't have to try to take me out."

"My bad. How are you? Are you in any pain?"

"A little bit. The doctors said that my brain function is good. My scars are healing and they want to send me home with a nurse within a couple of days. Sasha, I don't have a home to go to." Carmen's face turned sad.

"You can stay with me, Carmen, don't be like that."

"I can't do that. I couldn't invade you and your girls in that way. I'm gonna go by my mama's until I can get back on my feet. You know she has been lonely in her house since Ashlyn left with the kids."

"Are you sure?" Sasha asked.

"Yeah. It'll give my mama something to do with herself." Carmen laughed.

"I'm glad that you are okay. We have all been praying for you to get better. Lord knows it's been hell without you."

Carmen looked at Sasha and said, "I had a talk with Amekia. You may be mad but I told her how many times you came to my bedside to vent out your frustrations. I told her how you were hurt by her betrayal and that sooner or later y'all are gonna have to be cordial for y'all kids."

Sasha didn't know how to feel about Carmen telling Amekia what she had spoken to her about. She wanted to be furious, but what Carmen said she told Amekia made sense. Carmen was right. Sasha was getting too old to always be fighting Amekia when she saw her. She would rather suck up her emotions and deal with being around her for the sake of her girls, than to continuously get her ass whooped or whip Amekia's ass whenever they saw each other. Sasha said, "As much as I want to be mad at you for telling her what I told you, I can't be mad. I hate to admit it, but you are right and the kids is what's most important than anyone in this situation."

"Life is too short and I wish that just for the kids, y'all would and could just get along. Like I told her before she left, pray on it."

For the next hour and a half, Sasha and Carmen talked. Carmen told her how she was mad when she saw her burns for the first time while she was getting her bandages changed. Carmen told Sasha that she didn't have the proof, but she knew that Denise was involved somehow if she wasn't the one who set the fire herself. Sasha assured her that she would do everything in her power to take down everybody that was involved.

Sasha got up. "I'm about to get out of here. I gotta go get the girls from Brandon." She smoothed the wrinkles from her skirt, and kissed Carmen on her forehead.

"Wait. Before you go, how are you and Nas doing?" Carmen asked.

At the mention of his name and the thought of him, a smile spread across Sasha's face, but it quickly faded. She said, "I decided not to fuck with him. Did you know that he is Amekia's brother? How were we friends with her for so long and didn't know that she had a brother?"

"Amekia didn't have a great childhood, so I understand if she didn't want to divulge that situation. Her mother was a piece of shit, and Nas was already gone out of the house when things happened to her."

"What happened?"

"That's not my story to tell."

"But you could tell her that I was venting to you?" Sasha asked with a raised eyebrow.

"Not the same thing. What happened to her was horrible and if you knew, all those times you dug at her about sleeping with many men and telling her she would never find love, you would have never even said that shit to her when y'all were friends. Amekia is complicated and while what she did to you was wrong, she has a hurt soul. I don't think she intended for her and Brandon to sleep together. It was something that happened and continued to happen."

"Does that make it okay though?" Sasha asked.

"Of course not. And those are her demons to deal with. Somebody gotta be the bigger person in this situation."

"Carmen, why me though? I'm always the one who is being the bigger person!" Sasha exclaimed. It was the truth. She was always the one who had to apologize first or let bygones be bygones. She wasn't the one who was in the wrong, so why did she have to be the one to be the bigger person!

Carmen's eyes were beginning to become heavy. She was tired, and she knew this conversation wouldn't get anywhere with Sasha tonight. Sasha was level-headed and thought before her actions. Carmen knew that Sasha would think and rethink this situation over, so Carmen just decided to end the conversation. She said, "You are the bigger person because it is in your nature for you to be. You're gonna give this conversation some thought and decide to be the bigger person. Go home to your kids. Call Nas and apologize to him and talk to him about your feelings. Ain't nobody got time for you to be stuck in your feelings for a small part he played in this situation. Go get your man."

Sasha looked down at Carmen who had dismissed her with her eyes closed. She watched as her chest rose and fell. Carmen was knocked out due to the morphine drip that was connected to her I.V. Sasha shook her head and placed another kiss on her friend's forehead. On her way home, Sasha drove with her thoughts swimming, and picked up McDonald's for her girls. When she arrived home, she noticed Brandon's car in the driveway. She made a mental note to change the locks the following day. Climbing out of her car, she made her way to the front door and opened it. Brandon was in the kitchen, making the girls' dinner.

"Mommy!" Both of her girls yelled when she stepped into the living room.

"Hey, my babies. How was school?" Sasha asked, as she placed kisses on both of their heads.

With a pout on her face, thinking about what had happened in class, Aliana began: "It was fun. Except when Demarcus picked a booger and put it on Octavia. He made her cry."

"Boys are mean and disgusting when they are young. What the teacher do?" Sasha asked. She was disgusted at the thought of that little boy doing such a nasty thing. *He got one time to do some nasty shit to my baby, and I'm beating the breaks off his nappy headed ass mama,* Sasha thought to herself.

"She sent him to the office and he got a phone call home," Aliana said with laughter.

"Well, that's what he gets for doing that. That is not nice. If he bothers you, you tell me right away." Sasha winked.

Brandon came from the kitchen and said, "No, tell me first 'cause I got something special for little boys that make my girls cry."

Sasha's mouth dropped as his daughters laughed at him. After a moment of shock, Sasha said, "Brandon, don't tell them no shit like that. Hello, you forget I'm a damn lawyer."

Brandon shook his head as he stared at the side of Sasha's head. Sasha got up from the couch and proceeded to her bedroom to get undressed and bathe. Sasha didn't have the energy to deal with Brandon, so she decided to fill the tub up with steaming hot water, added her favorite peach scented bubble bath soap—and chamomile—to the water.

She turned the bathroom light off, and sunk into the tub, letting the heat from the water relax her muscles. Not even a full ten minutes went past before her phone dinged, indicating that she had a text message. Sighing, she reached over and grabbed her phone from the toilet.

Nas: Sasha, I miss you. Stop playing with a nigga and let him come see you.

A smile displayed on Sasha's face at the message. Even though the message was short, she couldn't help but smile because of the sweet tone behind the text. She missed Nas deeply. She didn't know what she was thinking when she told him that she couldn't fuck with him no more.

Sasha: I'm not gonna front like I don't miss you because I do. Things have just been really hectic lately.

Almost immediately after Sasha sent the text, Nas replied.

Nas: So, let me come over. I know our situation isn't the best but we can always work on making it better. I don't see you not being in my future Sasha and I just want to meet the girls and focus on us.

Things with Nas were different than what she had with Brandon. From the beginning of her and Brandon's relationship, it had felt like they had to uphold a certain appearance because both of their families were held with a certain prestige with the church. Since she was no longer with Brandon, Sasha was as free as she wanted to be without the watchful eye of her in-laws. With Nas, Sasha was absolutely comfortable with being herself. She never had to guess how Nas would look at her if she made a mistake. The only thing that stopped her from being with Nas the way that she wanted to was the fact that he was family with her number one enemy. *I need to get out of my own head and give this man a chance*, Sasha thought to herself as she looked at her phone screen. Nas had texted her three question marks when he noticed that she was taking too long to answer. Biting her bottom lip, she replied with a simple *okay*, and told him to give her an hour or two so that Brandon could continue to spend some time with his girls. When she put her phone down, she allowed her body to sink further into the tub until her chin touched the surface of the water.

***

Sasha stayed out of the way while Brandon fed the girls and put them to bed. Together with a glass of red wine, she ate the McDonald's she had bought them. She and Brandon barely spoke while he was there, and she was fine with that. She wanted him out so that she could prepare for Nas to come over. When Brandon left, she hurried up and locked up her house, placed the alarm on, and headed to her room to find something to put on. She settled on a red lace bralette and thong set from Savage Fenty, and placed biker shorts and a t-shirt over it. She placed her pink Nike slides on her feet, and sat in the living room, waiting for Nas to arrive.

Sasha was deep into an episode of *Blacklist*, and shit was just getting good when she heard a knock on the door. Pausing the show, she checked herself in the massive mirror on the wall in the living room, and proceeded to open the door. There was her man, looking edible. He was rocking a pair of light blue jeans, a black long-sleeved shirt, and black Timbs. A black fitted hat—with white *New York Yankee* etched on it—rested on his head.

"Hey," Sasha said shyly when her eyes made it to his.

Nas couldn't contain his smile. He bit his bottom lip before he broke out into a smile. Showing his white teeth, he said, "Damn! I almost forgot how beautiful you are."

"Cut it out. Cheesy ass line." Sasha gave a short laugh.

"Nah, you laughing but I'm being dead ass," Nas said with seriousness in his tone. Sasha moved to the side, and allowed Nas to enter her home. He stood off to the side, admiring her banging ass body while she closed and locked the door, making sure to also put the alarm on.

"You want something to drink?" Sasha asked.

"Yeah, let me just get some water for right now," Nas said, taking a seat on the sofa.

Trying to play like her heart wasn't pounding in her chest, she went to the kitchen to get him a cold bottled water.

They sat on the couch and watched the rest of the *Blacklist* episode. She felt Nasir looking at her several times, but didn't make a remark. She was nervous and didn't know why. She felt like this was her first time meeting him. *Girl, get yourself together—This is only Nas,* Sasha coached herself.

"Nas, I want to apologize for talking to you the way I did when I last spoke to you," Sasha started. Continuing, she said, "I never should have shut you out the way that I did. I was hurt behind all of the secrets that unfolded. I can't seem to get over the fact that you were related to Amekia."

"I know that this situation is wicked but my feelings for you, Sasha, are real. I feel bad about the part that I played in this, but nothing in this heart of mine is fake. I just want us to truly give us a chance and leave the past where it belongs."

"I want to. How do I put this shit behind me?" Sasha asked, casting her eyes to her lap. Carmen's words rang out in her head, as she looked over at Nas.

"We just gotta move one day at a time. I am in no rush. I want to get to know everything about you and I am sure even though you think you know a lot about me, you don't know the gentle side of me. You only saw a little bit, but I want to show you the gentleman that is in this beast." Nas was looking at her through slanted eyes.

"I hope that this shit doesn't bite me in the ass. I'm not even divorced yet and here I am entering the thought of another relationship."

"Look, ma, from what you told me, your relationship with Brandon was fucked up long before I entered the picture. Yeah, you still had love for the nigga, so you held on as long as you could to try to make it work. But ma, your mind was out the door way longer than your heart. Like I said, we don't have to rush anything. I'm intrigued with you and know that I'm not going anywhere until both of us are absolutely done with each other." Nas was serious. But he knew that the beef that Sasha and Amekia had was gonna have to be buried if they were going to work. He loved both women but for separate reasons, of course. If it really came down to it, he would choose his sister every time. When he found out from Amekia what happened to her when he left home, he felt like he failed her. All his father ever required of him was for him to protect his sister, whether he was around or not. And he failed. His loyalty and further protection was what he was providing for his sister. If Sasha ever made him choose, he was choosing Amekia.

"Okay," Sasha simply stated. Brandon moved on with his life way before she even found the proof that he was cheating, so she needed to do the same.

"Okay? That easy?" Nas asked, leaning closer to Sasha.

"Yes, that easy." She chuckled.

"Cool. Now I will have that drink. Make sure you take that bullshit off on your way back. Matter of fact, bring the whole bottle." Nas made this demand once Sasha had gotten up from her seat. She shook her head on the way to the kitchen. She did what her new man asked from her, and stripped out of her biker shorts and shirt, leaving them in the middle of the kitchen floor. She walked back with a sexy sway in her hips, and stood in front of Nas, who had begun to roll up his blunt. He looked up from breaking his weed up, and lusted over Sasha. If you didn't know Sasha, you would never know that she was a mother of two. She stood with her legs spread just enough for him to see the gap close to her vagina, with one hand on her hip and the other holding the neck of the bottle.

"You really want to finish rolling that up when you got all that you need right in front of you?" Sasha asked sexily.

Nas placed the weed back in its bag, and took the bottle from Sasha. He stood up in front of her, opened the bottle and took a swig. Because he was taller than her, he looked down into her eyes and placed a kiss on her lips. Sasha opened her mouth as she slid her tongue in his mouth, and he savored it. He ran his free hand up and down Sasha's neck as the kiss became a little heavy. Nas didn't know what it was about Sasha, but just the thought of her and the freaky things that she did, made his dick grow harder than it had ever been.

"Show me the way," Nas said in a husky voice. With a smile on her face, Sasha grabbed Nas' hand and walked him down to the basement door. Make up sex was the best sex to Sasha, and she knew that this session they were about to have could possibly wake up the girls. That's why she opted for the basement. As they descended downstairs, Nas turned the bottle up to his mouth.

Turning on the basement light, Sasha waltzed across the carpeted floor, and headed for the bar that was on the opposite side of the basement. She opened a bottle of Hennessy and poured herself a shot. She took it without hesitation, and followed up with another shot. Nas looked around the basement. He could tell that this was previously where her husband chilled. Everything about the basement screamed testosterone. He was going to enjoy fucking Sasha in a place where her husband used to enjoy. Nas walked over to Sasha, and took another swig. Her kitty got super wet at just the look he gave her. Placing his lips on hers, they kissed passionately again. Nas placed the bottle on top of the bar, and wrapped his arms around her waist. Faint moans escaped Sasha's lips when he lifted her up, and she swung her legs around his waist.

"I thought I wasn't going to ever see you," Nas whispered against Sasha's lips. He was serious too. The night they spoke in his car, he knew she was serious. Liquor will give you the courage to tell your mama her church wig was ugly and crooked. When she had gotten out of the car, he decided that he would give her some space, hoping that she would come around. When it didn't seem like she would, he took a leap on sending her the text, and she responded. He missed her like crazy, and was more than happy to see her.

Nas carried Sasha over to a ridiculously large bean bag chair, and carefully sat in it without dropping Sasha. She sat atop Nas, and looked at him through lust-filled eyes. She bit her bottom lip and removed the hair from her face. Nas took her bra off while she almost ripped his shirt off, causing them to laugh. Sasha leaned in close to Nas, and placed a kiss on his neck while rocking on his hard manhood that was begging to be released from the confinement of his boxers and jeans. Moving swiftly, Nas held Sasha's waist and flipped her onto her back on the bean bag. While he came out of his pants and boxers, Sasha teased Nas while pulling her lace thongs off her body. Dipping her finger between her slit, Sasha threw her head back, enjoying the pleasure her fingers were giving her.

"You gonna be selfish and not give ya man none of that gushy stuff?" Nas questioned.

With a smirk, Sasha said, "Come and get it."

Without having to say another word, Nas dropped into a squat and dragged Sasha closer to him, slightly bending her body so that just her head and shoulders were still on the bean bag. Nas took a deep whiff of her vagina, enjoying the peach scent mixed with a little tartness before he slid his thick tongue from her hole to her clit, and back around again. His tongue moved with expertise as he glided it up and down over her clit, creating the right amount of pressure to cause Sasha to almost instantly cum all over his tongue. He applied no mercy on her kitty as he sucked on her clit using his index and middle finger to move slowly in and out of her.

"Ooh Nas, I'm gonna cum." Sasha moaned as she used her thumb and index fingers to pinch and massage her nipples.

"Cum on this tongue then, baby. But when I stick this dick in you, I'm gonna need you to tell me that you cumming by saying that this my pussy. Can you do that for me?"

"Mmm. Yes, Nas."

"Then come on this tongue, baby," Nas said as he resumed flicking his tongue against her clit, causing Sasha to cum. She was spent after that, and wanted to roll over and get some rest. Nas had other plans, though. He lifted Sasha up so that he could sit on the bean bag chair. Nas' dick stood straight up, waiting for her kitty to slip onto it. Sasha climbed on top of Nas after he was comfortable. Placing his dick in her, she slid down slowly and paused when she felt all of him inside of her. Planting her feet on either side of his body, she bounced slowly while Nas grabbed her waist. He bit his bottom lip as Sasha slowly bounced on his dick with her eyes closed. *Damn! She is so fucking beautiful,* Nas thought to himself. Reaching his arms up, he palmed her breasts in his hands, causing Sasha to moan.

"Damn, girl!" Nas grunted out. He moved his hips to her rhythm as she picked up speed. He was trying to dig deep in her guts every time she slid down on his pole. Sasha was picking up speed. Nas had to admit to himself that he needed to get a grip on Sasha because she was getting serious about taking him on a ride. He wrapped his arm around her waist, and rotated his hips to make the head of his dick touch her stomach.

"I'm cumming, Nas. Ooh this your pussy, baby!" Sasha moaned out as her bouncing got faster.

"Cum on this dick, girl! Come on this fucking dick!" Nas grunted. He had pulled Sasha down close to his body as she moaned out. The orgasm that Sasha just experienced had her body shaking. Before she could catch her breath, she felt Nas flipping her over so that her ass was in the air and her back was arched. Nas fixed himself behind her, as he drilled into her like an animal. He was fucking her so good at one point she was breathless.

"I know you 'bout to come again. You might as well cum on this dick and let ya man cum with you." Nas growled in her ear. He was right about her cumming. Her body shook as he held onto her waist and plunged into her. Nas grunted as he leaked his seed inside of her.

"Oh shit, Nas! Mmm." Sasha moaned. Soon as they came, Sasha collapsed onto the bean bag while Nas laid on top of her. Neither said a thing to each other as they tried to regain their composure.

"You okay?" Nas asked.

“Yeah, I’m okay. You?” Sasha replied while rolling onto her side.

“Now I’m good,” Nasir responded as he closed his eyes. Before either of them knew it, they had fallen into a slumber. Good sex will do the trick every single time.

Chapter Nine

"Mama, I'm fine. Would you stop fussing over me?" Carmen complained as she watched her elderly mother move about the room, making sure that her eldest daughter was comfortable. It had been two weeks since Carmen had been released from the hospital. She was on her way to recovery, and was doing so at a rapid pace. She had a surgery coming up in a couple of days for one of the burns on the back of her leg, and her doctor was sure that she would be as good as new. Of course, she would have scars but her burns so far didn't look too bad.

"Oh, girl, hush. I'm just trying to make sure that when that fine ass nurse gets here, he will feel welcomed." Ms. Bowden fussed. Carmen had to admit, the nurse that the hospital assigned her was a cutie. He was tall, well over six feet if she had to guess. He had deep chocolate brown skin that was blemish-free, with deep waves that would make anyone seasick if they looked too hard, and he had the shiniest full beard on his face. To Carmen he resembled Kofi Siriboe.

"Mama, you're making it seem like he's coming here to see you. He doesn't want you." Carmen chuckled as she watched her mother go into the kitchen and start preparing lunch.

"You never know. I haven't had a man since your no good ass daddy left, and that young thing might just be what I need." Ms. Bowden spoke as she took out items to make cold cut sandwiches.

"First of all, my daddy died. You are making it seem like he left you for another woman. And second, eww. I'm sure he doesn't want your cobwebbed coochie."

"You watch your tongue now. Just because I am lusting over a man doesn't mean that I don't have Jesus in my heart. You might want to watch me work my magic when that young man arrives. You might learn a thing or two."

Carmen almost wanted to throw up in her mouth. She said, "Mama, ain't lusting a sin?"

"Jesus knows my heart," Ms. Bowden said, and followed it up by humming a gospel song. Carmen shook her head at her mother. She didn't know what to do with that lady. Some days she was holy and sanctified; other days she was a thot box, and it was wearing Carmen's nerves. Carmen couldn't wait until she was able to find a place so that she could leave her mother's home. She loved her mother, but all this fussing over her was getting annoying. Besides wanting to get out of her mother's house, she couldn't wait to see Denise. She knew that Denise was behind the fire, and she needed to come up with a plan and somehow get a recording of her confession to the deed. When her mother wasn't in her face making sure that she was okay, she was thinking of a plan to execute.

Ding! Dong!

The sound of the doorbell ringing brought Carmen back to reality. Just as she was about to get up from off the couch to answer her door, she saw her mother rushing to the mirror on the wall to make sure her good wig was on straight. Carmen couldn't help herself, and she busted out in laughter. She laughed so hard that she sat back onto the couch holding her stomach.

"What are you laughing so hard for? Go answer the door for my future husband and your future step daddy." Ms. Bowden huffed. Shaking her head, Carmen slowly got up from off the couch, and made her way to the door. She hated to admit that she was just as excited as her mother to see this man. He was a good distraction from what she was dealing with lately.

When she opened the door, there he was in all of his glorious handsomeness, dressed in powder blue scrubs with his small duffel bag filled with items that he needed for the day. Carmen placed a smile on her blushing face and said, "Hey. Come on in."

"Thank you," he simply responded. Zaquan was always professional when he came, and at times Carmen hated it. He never flirted with her, even though she did it subtly at times. However, her mother had done it with no shame and all he ever did was, laugh at it.

"Is that Zaquan?" Her mother yelled from the kitchen, knowing damn well it was. Carmen rolled her eyes before she answered. Zaquan caught it and lightly chuckled.

"Yes, mama, it is," she responded.

"I will be right out with lunch. Your trifling sister called me to go pick up my grandbabies from school in a little while. They asked her to work a double."

"Okay, mama."

Ms. Bowden walked out of the kitchen just as Zaquan had started to change Carmen's bandages. He said, "You're healing very well, Miss. Bowden. Every day there is less blood on these bandages and that is a good sign. Soon I should be out of your hair. How is the pain?"

"It comes and goes but when it's here it's extremely painful. I get through it sometimes without having to take Tylenol."

"Which is good and means that you aren't being dependent on it. Sometimes people get dependent on it and your body adjusts to it and won't work at all. And that is how some people get addicted to opioids. They look for something that is stronger and usually a doctor begins to prescribe narcotics, creating a bad habit. I am glad that you are doing fine with just Tylenol. You have no idea how many people I see get hooked on opioids because they can't or won't allow themselves to deal with the pain." Carmen understood what he was saying. That was one of the reasons why she tried to deal with the pain without taking anything for it. She smoked weed a time or two, but that was it. She refused to be dependent on any kind of drug. She saw what drugs did to people's minds and appearance, and neither of those she wanted to lose. She thanked God for her willpower.

"It's sad to see all these young folks walking around here looking half dead," Ms. Bowden said as she watched Zaquan closely.

Both Carmen and Zaquan nodded in agreement with Ms. Bowden. Zaquan was focusing on a scar that Carmen had on her leg that didn't look too good. It was more red than it had been the past two days, and from what Zaquan saw, it looked like it was getting infected. Zaquan asked, "Ms. Bowden, do you have a foot soaker or a bucket?"

"I do actually. What's going on?" Carmen's mother asked.

"It looks like this burn may be starting to become infected. I just want to clean this better with soap and water. I am also going to let your doctor know to prescribe you something for the infection. Has this burn been giving you any pain?"

"Zaquan, when I'm in pain, my whole body hurts so I can't pinpoint that one being a primary," Carmen said. Her mother came back with some warm water in a foot soaker, and decided to leave the house to pick up her grandchildren. Zaquan removed Carmen's sock from her foot, and softly placed her foot inside of the soaker. She leaned her head back, enjoying the warmth of the water. Taking a fresh soft sponge from his bag, Zaquan put it in the water and squeezed the water from it across her burn. Next, he took out a bar of antibacterial soap and lathered it onto the sponge.

"Your mother is on a trip, you know that?" Zaquan stated.

"She only acts like that when you come around." Carmen chuckled.

"For some reason, I believe it."

"You should. She gets all hot and bothered when she knows that you are about to be on your way. She thinks you are about to be her new husband and all."

"Women like your mother are the reason why I love my job. They don't sugar-coat anything and they feed me. Women your age—man, they see me and instead of focusing on their treatment plan, they want to get into my pants." Zaquan laughed.

Carmen understood where the women were coming from. Zaquan was easy on the eye. She cracked a smile and said, "Yeah, I can see how they can easily lose focus. I know you are here to do a job but the nursing agency you with know what they are doing by keeping you employed."

Zaquan looked at Carmen like she was crazy, but couldn't hold his laughter back. He fell onto his ass and hollered at what Carmen stated. When he got his nerve together, he looked at her and said, "You trying to say that they only keeping me because of my looks?"

"I mean if it walks like a duck—shit, you know how the rest go. You are a very handsome man and I'm sure that the majority of your clients are women."

As Zaquan thought about it, he knew that Carmen was doing nothing but speaking facts. He nodded as he said, "Yeah, you're right. Damn, I never even thought about it like that. I just come to do my job and go home. The flattery is always welcomed, though. Just like women, men love to be complimented as well. Some more than others. I'm some."

Carmen laughed. She said, "Well, at least you're honest about the shit."

The room got quiet, as Zaquan attentively picked Carmen's foot and placed it on the towel that laid across his knee. Reaching down inside of the bag that was by his foot, he took out a topical antibacterial cream and put some on the tips of his fingers, before rubbing gently across the inflamed burn. Carmen had to admit that it felt good and relaxing. She closed her eyes as Zaquan continued to cover the burn up with gauze and tape. She honestly hadn't realized that the particular burn had caused her pain.

"Okay. Your burns are all good. I'm gonna call your doctor now to see if he could send a prescription of penicillin to the pharmacy. You need anything before I make this call?" Zaquan asked. He had to hurry up and get out of that house. Carmen let a few moans escape her mouth while he was tending to her burn. It got him excited. He saw himself placing her pretty small toes in his mouth, and that's when he decided to wrap up what it was he was doing.

"No. You know if there is anything I need, I will get up and get the shit myself. I'm healing, not dying!" Carmen snidely stated. She hated whenever anyone was over, they would always ask if she needed anything. She never wanted to be treated like a handicap, and that is exactly how everyone treated her. She may have moved slow, but she was more than willing and able to fetch herself whatever it was she needed. Zaquan nodded and made his way into the kitchen to make the phone call. Carmen picked up the remote, took one half of a sandwich her mother made, and turned on Netflix to catch up on *Shameless*.

When Zaquan entered the room again, Carmen ignored him. She was still salty as a result of him asking her if she needed anything. Truth be told, he felt like he allowed that question to slip through his full set of lips. He knew she was independent; she made that shit clear from jump, but he was nervous and he wanted to put distance between them. He took a seat on the other end of the couch that Carmen was on. He grabbed the other half of the sandwich and sat back to watch *Shameless* with Carmen.

When the show ended and was on its way to the next episode, Zaquan picked up the remote and paused it. Carmen sat up on the couch, and looked at Zaquan as if she wanted to kill him. Before she spoke, Zaquan held his hands up in surrender and said, “Whoa, relax. I’m only pausing it so that I can apologize to you. I know that you are independent, but you have to remember that I also have clients who aren’t and it’s always gonna slip out from time to time. I didn’t mean to offend you.”

Carmen looked at Zaquan and wondered if he was being sincere. The look in his eyes told her so. She knew he had other clients, some of them even being older. Her face softened, and she realized that she was being a bitch for absolutely no reason. She softened her brows and said, “I’m sorry.”

Zaquan wasn’t expecting for Carmen to apologize. He looked on in confusion, as Carmen turned her head back to the TV and pressed *play* on the remote. Shrugging, he chose to remain quiet for the rest of the time that he was there. When he made sure that Carmen was straight, he walked out of the house and happily made his way home.

Later on that night, when Carmen was lying awake in bed, she thought about the burn that was inflamed and on its way to infection. She lied to Zaquan about her use of pain medication. She was in fact taking Vicodin that her sister got from her boyfriend. Not only did the Vicodin take away any pain that she was feeling, but it also put her in a euphoric state that she didn't want to leave alone. In that state, she didn't have a care in the world. She didn't feel the pain of her burns, and she sometimes forgot that she even had any burns. She tried with everything in her to fight the urge of reaching into the drawer of her nightstand that held the Vicodin. Carmen effortlessly tried to fall asleep, but the medication kept calling her name. She tossed and turned for twenty minutes before she opened the drawer, and the pills sang out to her. Her mouth watered as she reached all the way to the back of the drawer and pulled out the pills that were nestled inside some napkins. Opening the napkin, her mouth salivated. She was soon going to have to get more. She was down to six from the twenty that she had gotten two weeks ago when she had gotten home. Ashlyn didn't ask her older sister what she needed the Vicodin for; she knew for a fact that her sister had to be in pain because of the accident. So when Carmen asked her if she knew anybody that could get her something strong for her pain, Ashlyn didn't ask any questions.

Carmen grabbed two pills from the napkin, and took them with just her saliva, forcing them down. Wrapping the other pills up, she laid back and waited for the drug to do its job.

Chapter Ten

Three Months Later

It took Amekia months for Brandon to convince her to allow their daughter to go to daycare and for her to return to work. After Amekia's mother kidnapped her daughter, she didn't trust a soul around her daughter, and she didn't want to put her in an unsafe environment so that she wouldn't go missing again. Amekia knew that she had to go back to work, which was the only reason why she agreed to put Aziyah in a daycare. Her baby was growing fast, and Aziyah was about turning one, and would soon be trying to walk. Amekia was surprised at how fast her baby was picking up on things at seven months old. She had her crawling down and every chance she got she wanted her parents to put her on the floor so that she could move about. The only thing was that Aziyah hadn't caught onto the fact that she needed both of her legs to crawl. So, her crawling was her using one knee and both hands to navigate while her other leg was just dragged on the ground. Amekia had concerns, but Aziyah's doctor told her not to worry, adding that pretty soon she would be using both of her legs.

Amekia looked down at her watch, as she sat at the nurses' desk, completing inventory for the office. She had twenty more minutes, and then she was out of there and picking up her baby. Like any other parent, she missed her baby. This being apart from her was something that would take a while for her to get used to. Amekia wrapped up her duties, and headed straight to the break room to grab her things from her locker. On the way out, she stopped by the office of the dentist that she was under, and asked if she needed anything before she left. Dr. Jackson couldn't have said *No* fast enough. Before she even got the full word out of her mouth, Amekia was racing down the hallway and out the door to go get her baby.

After grabbing Aziyah from daycare, Amekia stopped at the local grocery store to grab something to make for dinner. As she picked up items to make lamb chops, she thought about her relationship with Brandon. After Aziyah was born and Amekia allowed Brandon to come over to visit Aziyah, he never left. Slowly, he brought clothes over and the next thing Amekia knew, he had planted himself in her spare bedroom. Amekia didn't mention him being sneaky and moving in; she knew that if she did, he would feel somehow. He was a big help around the house and with Aziyah; she would be a fool to bring that up to him, and he'd end up deciding to leave. She would be a plumb fool.

Amekia made it home just a little after five-thirty and immediately put Aziyah in her jump-and-learn bouncer, and headed to the kitchen. Taking everything out of the bags, she quickly seasoned the lamb chops, and made a marinade from garlic, thyme, rosemary, and olive oil. She placed that in the fridge to marinate for an hour, and moved onto preparing her daughter for bed. Amekia laughed every time it was time for Aziyah to go to bed. It was because of Brandon that her daughter was this way. She was going to be a handful once she got a boyfriend.

Boiling water on the stove, Amekia looked through the many jars of baby food that Aziyah had, and decided on feeding her growing baby sweet potato turkey with a whole grain dinner made by Gerber. Placing the jar in the boiling water, she turned the water off and let it sit while she went to make a five ounce bottle of formula. Aziyah knew it was time for her to eat, and she began to fuss. Amekia sped up the process with getting her baby girl's food ready. Taking her shoes off by the door, she picked up Aziyah and brought her to her high chair in the kitchen to feed her. An hour and a half later, Amekia had fed Aziyah, gave her a warm bath, and topped her off with a nice warm bottle of milk. Aziyah was now asleep and in her crib. Closing the door half way as she exited, Amekia sighed in relief as she headed into her room. She took off her clothes, placed her robe on, and went into the kitchen to cook the lamb chops, mashed potatoes and gravy, and oven-roasted garlic parmesan asparagus.

When dinner was done, Amekia placed the food on top of warmers on the table. Thereafter, she went to take a shower. While Amekia was at work, she had thought about all of the shit that Brandon had done and proved over the past few months, and she felt just saying thank you wasn't enough to show her appreciation for him. By cooking dinner, she figured that would show him appreciation. When Amekia got out of the shower, she noticed that Brandon had texted her, letting her know that he was on his way. She quickly got dressed in black runner shorts, a wife beater with no bra, and thigh-high black socks. She was thankful that Aziyah didn't cause her boobs to sag. She was thankful that she was even able to wear a beater without a bra, and they still sat up nice and perky just like before she had her baby.

Amekia sat nervously at the table while she waited for Brandon to come home. She tried to get rid of her nervousness by scrolling through Instagram, but that did nothing but make her jittery. Give or take, fifteen minutes passed, and she had finally heard Brandon coming through the door. At that moment, Amekia tried to remember at what point in her life did she give that man a key. She was going to bring it up, but not that night. She listened as he dropped his keys on the table that was close to the front door.

"What the fuck smell so damn good? Amekia, where you at?" Brandon called out. He knew that Aziyah was asleep, and didn't want to wake her with his yelling. He just hoped that Amekia was somewhere on the bottom level of the house to hear him.

"In the kitchen!" she called out. Her palms were sweating as his footsteps neared her.

Brandon looked around the kitchen, and zeroed in on Amekia. She sat at the table with a smile on her face. He raised his eyebrow and said, "Please don't tell me that you planning on poisoning me."

Amekia scrunched her face up and said, "I should be because how the fuck you get a key if I never gave you one? But that's not here nor there. No, I'm not poisoning you. I just wanted to show my appreciation for you. You have been more than a big help to both me and Aziyah, and I figured after working all day, you would appreciate a nice quiet dinner."

Brandon eyed Amekia. He appreciated that she did this for him. All the same, he felt it wasn't necessary. What she didn't know was that Brandon was in love with her, and he would go above and beyond for her. A smile crept onto his face as Amekia broke their eye contact by beginning to fix his plate. He began, "It's about damn time that you started to recognize all the work that I do around here."

"Brandon, don't fucking push it," Amekia stated, as she rolled her eyes.

"Alright, alright. I'm sorry. Thank you for this." Brandon stood behind her and wrapped his arms around her for a hug. Amekia's body became rigid, yet she did not want to pass the wrong impression. She soon relaxed because it had been forever since she was held, even if it was just a hug. As soon as the hug started and before she got too comfortable,

Brandon moved away from her to go wash his hands and face before he dug in. Amekia fanned herself as soon as Brandon walked out of the kitchen. She just wanted them to enjoy their dinner, not get hot and bothered by her baby daddy.

When Brandon returned, Amekia was piling food onto his plate and grabbing his glass to fill it up with cold bottled water. He smiled as she moved about how she used to before he had gotten her pregnant. He was lost in his thoughts when she placed his plate in front of him and sat down in her own seat.

"Penny for your thoughts?" Amekia questioned.

Before Brandon answered, he placed some mashed potatoes and asparagus in his mouth, savoring it. Finally, he said, "I was just remembering how our relationship was before you had Aziyah."

"You mean before your wife found out?" Amekia huffed. Their relationship before wasn't what she was too fond of discussing. She just wanted to eat and shower.

"Yes. But that was also before you had Aziyah. I was with Sasha physically but you had me physically, mentally, and emotionally."

"That's not how it was supposed to be, Brandon. We were just supposed to be fucking. I love Aziyah and couldn't have asked for a better child, but the situation was just sticky, and we shouldn't have even let it get that far."

Brandon let her words marinate in his mind. He agreed with her, but he knew deep down inside that she did love him. They'd had no time to talk about what happened, and he was glad to be able to do it now. He looked at Sasha and said, "You can't tell me that you didn't love me."

"I do. I mean I did, Brandon, but I knew that you would never be mine, so the best option was to just be fuck buddies." Amekia shrugged.

Brandon paused before he asked his next question. The way she was talking, there was a possibility that she could turn him down. He said, "Amekia, I have been thinking lately. And this may be a stretch, but I want us to try for a relationship. I've known for a while that I loved you, but I have no doubts that I am in love with you. I don't want another female the way I want you. Our relationship made sense to me, and with me getting a divorce, I'd like it if we could actually try."

Amekia looked at Brandon to see if he was serious. From the look on his face, she noticed that he was really serious. Amekia didn't know how to respond to what Brandon wanted. She wasn't sure if she felt the same way. Sure, she loved him. He gave her a baby, so she would always love him. But to say that she wanted to work on an intimate relationship with him when they needed to work on being parents to their child—that was a whole new ball game.

"Brandon I—"

"It's nothing that you need to give me an answer on now. I just want you to know that it's where I'm at."

Amekia shut her mouth and got quiet. If this would have been when he was still with Sasha, she wouldn't have entertained him trying to be with her. In the past, Amekia would have denied him harder than a prostitute bouncing on a dick for money. She was cool with their situationship but now, she didn't know what she would do. Several times, Amekia thought that when her mother took Aziyah, it was her karma for sleeping with Brandon. Although there was a time or two since he had been there that she thought about what they could possibly be, but instantly would get the thought out of her head. Amekia swirled her fork in her mashed potatoes, and looked up at Brandon. He was staring her down, and the heat from his stare was flushing on her cheeks.

Brandon placed his fork on his plate, and got up from the table. Amekia exhaled, relieved that he was leaving from the table. Amekia placed her fork on her plate, and sat back in her seat with her eyes closed. *I need to get my feelings in check,* she thought to herself. Just as she was about to clear the table of the barely eaten food, she felt Brandon's hand on her face. He was stroking her face tenderly. She looked up into Brandon's eyes. He stared at her for a few moments and then bent down, placing a kiss on her lips. His plan was to leave the table to give her some time to process what he had said, but when she leaned back in her chair, with her eyes closed in defeat, he had decided to go over. It was crazy to him that his heart was beating for her when it didn't even beat for his wife when he was with her.

Amekia opened her mouth, savoring his tongue in her mouth. Instantly, moisture pooled into the seat of her panties. There was passion in the kiss but also something new. Amekia could feel it because she had never felt a kiss like this from him before. Brandon's hand rested on her neck, as he lightly squeezed. His dick was rock-hard in his pants, but there was something in him that was animalistic. All he wanted at that moment was to slam into Amekia and make her scream in pleasure. However, they didn't have the house to themselves, and their daughter was upstairs sleeping, so passionate lovemaking would have to do. That is, if she didn't stop him.

Amekia reached up and caressed his face as she tried to get up from her seat, trying not to break the kiss they were sharing. When she stood from her seat, they broke the kiss.

Brandon took her hand into his, as they made their way into the living room. Brandon sat on the couch, and he brought her down onto his lap. Blushing, Amekia sat on his lap and placed her lips over his. His dick pressed into her pussy, making it thump in anticipation. As they kissed, Brandon slid his hand into her shorts and slipped his finger into her moistness. She allowed a moan to escape her lips against his, and his fingers swirled against her clit.

"Shit," Brandon whispered against her lips. He was ready to feel her pussy while wrapped around her folds. When she came against his fingers, he pulled her shorts over her hips, and freed himself from his pants. After a moment's thought, he moved her away from his lap and pulled his pants down to his ankles. When Amekia was back on his lap, she unbuttoned his shirt and ran her hands across his chest and abs. Reaching his arms around her body, he lifted her up by her ass cheeks and sat her on his dick. Amekia moaned as she slid down his dick. It had been so long since she had dick that she almost came the instant the head of his dick entered her. Planting her feet on either side of his legs, she slowly bounced up and down. Brandon lifted her shirt up off her breasts, causing them to spill out into his face. Instantly, his mouth wrapped around her nipple as he met her thrusts.

"Oooh shit, Brandon. I think I'm gonna cum already!" Amekia moaned only moments of being on top of him.

"This your dick girl, cum all you want." With those simple words, Amekia came on his dick, wetting up his pelvis, dick, and balls. When she was done, Brandon helped her as he leaned her back onto the wooden coffee table that sat in the middle of the room. He climbed on top of her, and moved as if it was going to be his last stroke game he gets to put down. Amekia moaned in delight, as he tugged at her hair and placed kisses on her neck.

"Ohh Brandon!" Amekia moaned.

"I was serious about being your man, Amekia. It's crazy—shit—how my heart beats for you. It's crazy how I can't even begin to picture my life without you. You already let me put a baby in you, so give me a chance and let me be your man—fuck." Brandon whispered those words into her ear. She never thought that the words he spoke would make her pussy wetter, but here she was, and the only sound in the room—besides their heavy panting—was her pussy talking loudly.

"But what if—"

"Ain't no what if's, babe. I promise I won't ever do you how I did Sasha. What we got ain't nothing like what I had with Sasha. Just tell your man yes."

While it all sounded good, there was something in the back of her mind screaming: *The way you got him is the way you lose him.* But her heart won when her mind screamed *no*. Looking into Brandon's eyes, she saw the sincerity and love as she nodded by way of saying yes. That's when Brandon let the beast lose. He balanced himself on top of her, his hands near her head, his feet on the ground, and her legs in the air. He pounded into her, causing the coffee table to shake underneath their weight. Amekia hollered as if he was killing her. Well, technically, he was killing her pussy. His balls slapped against her ass cheeks, as he felt his nut building up. He would usually go longer, but it had been a while since he was in some pussy, and he was ready to nut.

"I'm not on birth control," Amekia managed to grunt out. Brandon was almost there, and was enjoying her pussy. They didn't need another baby just yet, and he beat himself up for not putting a condom on. As much as he didn't want to, Brandon pulled out, giving him time to prolong his release.

Wiping sweat from his brow, he stood up and said, “Play in your pussy.”

With a confused expression, Amekia did what he asked. She bent her knees and swirled her fingers in her gushiness. Brandon walked to the end of the table, where her head rested as he stroked himself. Brandon leaned over her head and played with her nipples. Amekia was working on her third orgasm as she watched Brandon stroke himself. She loved watching Brandon stroke himself, and he knew this. In seconds, she was cumming again. He stood up and released on her face and chest.

“Damn, you a whole porn star in this bitch. And that’s what I love about you.” Brandon huffed as he took a seat on the couch. Amekia rolled off the table with laughter, and sat next to Brandon. The sound of banging on the front door stilled both of them as Aziyah screeched.

“Get the door. I’ma go get Aziyah. Whoever has the nerve to come banging on the door waking up my baby getting cursed out.” Amekia spat those words as she walked to go get the baby. She dressed as she moved. While Brandon wanted the unwanted guest to leave, he knew they wouldn’t. Whoever it was meant business, by the sound of the rushed knocks. Brandon left his shirt off, but pulled his pants on and went to go answer the door. He was surprised to see Amekia’s brother on the other end, and he could tell that Nas was just as surprised as he was.

“Nas, I’m gonna fuck you up knocking on my door like that. You woke Aziyah up and it’s gonna take forever for me to get her back to sleep!” Amekia fussed. Nas sidestepped Brandon, inviting himself in with a mean mug on his face.

“Yeah, all that, sis. I’m glad both ya’ll niggas is here ‘cause I need to say something to y’all,” Nas said as he made his way into the living room. He paused when he entered and sniffed the air, causing Amekia and Brandon to look at each other and laugh.

"What is so important that you had to wake my baby up instead of just fucking call?" Amekia asked, as she tried to stop laughing at the look on his face.

"I regret not calling," Nas said as he left the room and went into the kitchen. Both Brandon and Amekia continued to laugh as they followed Nas into the kitchen.

"Y'all laughing now, but when y'all got a million and fifty kids running around here, I don't want to hear shit about no Uncle Nas. Now if y'all done skinning and grinning, I would like to speak to you both." Nas eyed his sister and Brandon with his face etched in seriousness.

"Wait, is everything okay?" Amekia asked, recognizing the look on Nas' face.

"Yeah, everything is okay. I just wanted y'all to know that I am in a relationship with Sasha, and I need for you to be cool with Sasha, and I'm gonna respect you as a man and do my best with being cordial with you." Nas spoke directly, looking at both Brandon and Amekia.

"I know like hell you didn't come banging on my door to tell me that bullshit," Amekia said, instantly becoming irritated.

"Amekia, chill. I can respect where he coming from. I appreciate you coming. I can agree with you by being cordial. At the end of the day—"

Amekia interrupted: "Nah, I don't respect it."

Brandon turned to Amekia and gave her a stern look that told her to chill. He said, "Amekia, how can you not? We just made the decision to work on our relationship and we didn't begin to think about mentioning it to anyone."

"That's 'cause it ain't nobody business!" Amekia snapped.

"It is when your brother is with my ex-wife and I'm with his sister. Chill out. Nobody said that you had to talk to Sasha, just be cordial. I do have kids with her and our child is their sibling. Everybody adults, so it shouldn't have to be like nobody can get along." When Brandon finished talking, Nas looked over at Amekia with a smirk on his face. Amekia caught the smirk and turned her attention towards him.

"Ain't shit funny with your goofy ass. I'm gonna listen to my man—emphasis on *my man,* but I don't want to hear about shit when you think about cheating 'cause she ain't giving you no pussy." Amekia grabbed Aziyah's bottle from the bottle warmer, and walked out of the kitchen. Brandon shook his head as she walked away. Brandon would have to suck it up and be the clear-headed one. Brandon could accept Nas coming to them. It wasn't a permission thing, it was more so to let them know what they were on.

Brandon turned towards Nas and stuck his hand out to dap up Nas. When Nas grabbed his hand, Brandon said, "I appreciate you coming. I'll try to get your sister to come around on accepting you and Sasha being together."

"Nah, you don't have too. We are all grown and I'm gonna be with Sasha no matter who likes it or not. I only came to tell her, 'cause I didn't know that you were going to be here. Y'all niggas was wrong in the situation."

"You don't own up to how you played in it?" Brandon asked, looking at Nas with a side eye.

"Nah, I admitted it. But that was to Sasha and that was the one who mattered. She knows that I gave her those papers on request from Amekia. There ain't no reason as to why I need to lie to her anymore. I love that woman, bruh, and there won't never ever be another time where I lie to her. I'm gonna one day meet your girls and I want to assure you that I will protect all of them with everything in me." Nas was confident, and Brandon respected that.

Brandon nodded in understanding. He said, "I appreciate it."

Nas and Brandon dapped each other, and Nas decided to go. He told Brandon to tell Amekia he loved her and would be in touch soon. When the door was locked, Brandon went into the living room and cleaned up the mess that he and Amekia made. By the time he was done, Amekia had gotten Aziyah back to sleep and began cleaning the kitchen up. Amekia's mind was on what her brother told her. She knew she was being irrational about the situation, but she didn't care. Nas wasn't supposed to fall for Sasha. He was just supposed to be a pawn to keep her occupied until she wanted to reveal the paper trail.

"Amekia." Brandon spoke, breaking Amekia's thoughts.

"Huh?" She answered, looking up from washing the dishes.

"You didn't hear me?"

"Nah. I was thinking. What did you say?"

"I said it's still a little early, did you want to watch something?" Brandon asked, raising his eyebrow in suspicion.

"Oh yeah, sure. Let me just finish cleaning the kitchen and we could watch something." Amekia smiled.

Brandon smiled back and walked away, thinking to himself: *For once I hope my life could be semi-normal. I don't need no more drama. Amekia is it for me.* After Amekia was done with the kitchen, she met Brandon in the living room. They chose to watch *Ray*, a film starring Jamie Foxx. It was their favorite movie together. Not too long after the movie started, Amekia was curled up under Brandon's arm, sleeping. Brandon didn't care that she fell asleep. After all, he did just blow her back out. As long as she was content, he was fine with her falling asleep on their movie.

Chapter Eleven

Carmen sat on the couch while her mother was in the kitchen preparing for Thanksgiving the next day. Since Carmen was still having issues with her wounds, Mrs. Bowden thought it would be a good idea to have Carmen's friends over. She also invited Zaquan, her daughter's nurse; he declined but she almost begged for him to come over. He agreed, but she knew that would be pushing it. He had a family to spend the holidays with, and she could only imagine that he wanted to spend all of his holiday with them.

Carmen's habit with percs was becoming stronger by the day. She told herself that there was nothing wrong with her using them for the pain. At least that's what her brain made her think. She was hooked without even knowing. Before she came downstairs to join her mother, she got a good look in the mirror and didn't like what stared back at her. Her eyes were rimmed red and baggy. She hadn't been able to sleep a wink in forty-eight hours. She didn't want her mother to question her. She applied make-up, and placed shades over her eyes. She was sure that her mother would say something about her wearing shades in the house because she was old-school like that.

"Carmen, can you come in here and help peel these potatoes for this salad?" Mrs. Bowden called from the kitchen.

Pausing the movie she was watching, she replied: "Sure, mama, I'm coming."

It had been a while since her mother had cooked a huge Thanksgiving dinner, and Carmen knew that her mother was excited and in her element. This Thanksgiving would be a little different because Carmen's sister was dating a guy who was serious about her. He stepped in and became a step dad to her children, and he invited Ashlyn to his family's house in Ohio, where he was originally from.

"Girl, why the hell you got the damn glasses on here?" Mrs. Bowden asked, when she saw Carmen sitting at the table peeling the already boiled potatoes.

"Mama, I didn't get any sleep last night and my eyes hurt with all these lights on." Carmen pouted and fussed.

Mrs. Bowden placed her hand on her hip and gave Carmen a stern look. Just because Carmen was an adult didn't mean that the look didn't work on her. Hell, that look had been correcting Carmen since she was able to understand what the look meant. Carmen sighed and took her glasses off without a protest. She didn't expect mother's reaction and when she got it, it made her feel small. The gasp that her mother took told Carmen that she was rather surprised at her appearance. Mrs. Bowden, after realizing that her mouth was hanging open, simply closed it and turned back around to the sink. *What the hell is going on with my child, Lord? That is not what not having sleep looks like,* Mrs. Bowden thought to herself. Collecting herself before she spoke, she turned around to face Carmen again. Carmen's chin was in her chest and tears were streaming down her face.

Mrs. Bowden squatted in front of her daughter and cupped her thumb and index finger under her chin, forcing Carmen to look at her. She said, "I got it. Go get some rest. The next time I see you, I know like hell you better not look like this."

Carmen nodded and got up from the table. Before she fully walked out of the kitchen, her mother grabbed her hand and stood on her tiptoe, placing a kiss on her forehead. Carmen walked away, wanting to release a bloodcurdling scream. For a split second, disgust registered on her mother's face, and she had caught it. It was right before her mother had turned to the sink. It caused her heart to shatter. One thing Carmen never wanted was for her mother to look at her with disgust. However, with a budding addiction taking over, Carmen accomplished just that reaction from her mom.

***

Stretching her stiff limbs, Carmen slowly opened her eyes. Her mouth and throat was dry, and her eyes felt swollen. The sun was shining bright, causing Carmen to smile. She had gotten an hour of sleep, and it had been the best hour that she had ever had. Grabbing her towel, wash rag, and body wash, she made her way into the bathroom for a shower. Setting the temperature of the shower to the hottest, she began to brush her teeth. She looked at herself in the mirror, and was pleased about that little bit of sleep she had gotten. With a smile, she climbed into the shower and washed herself real good.

Carmen made sure that she didn't stay in the shower for too long. Her mother had to know that she was up. She didn't want her to wait on her to come downstairs. Carmen dressed in a pair of flannel pajama pants and a regular white tee. With slippers on her feet, she made her way to the living room. Her mother wasn't there, and when she smelled the scent of food being cooked, she went to the kitchen. Just like she knew, her mother was moving about the kitchen, cooking.

"Hey, mama," Carmen greeted. Mrs. Bowden turned away from the stove with a smile on her face.

"Happy Thanksgiving, baby," Mrs. Bowden replied.

Carmen looked at her mother strangely as if she had lost her mind. She said, "Mama, maybe you need to get some rest. It's still Wednesday."

Mrs. Bowden shook her head and looked at Carmen. She said, "Check your phone, sweetheart. It's Thanksgiving Day."

Carmen's face fell when she checked her phone. Besides the missed text messages that she had gotten from her friends, there it was; clear as day. *I must have really needed that sleep. I slept for almost eighteen hours. Jeez! No wonder I felt so refreshed.* Without another word, Carmen replied to her friends, wishing each of them Happy Thanksgiving. Sasha instantly responded when she had received the text, to tell Carmen that she couldn't make it. She didn't give a reason, but Carmen knew more than anything that the reason Sasha wasn't coming for Thanksgiving dinner was because of Amekia. Frankly, Carmen was done with the drama between them, and was glad that one of them was staying behind. She just wanted to have a peaceful night with her girls.

Mrs. Bowden busied herself as Carmen laid her phone down on the table. She reached into the pantry, and grabbed a few pots and pans in order to help her mother. Carmen was grateful to be alive, and she wasn't about to spend unnecessary time on stupid shit. For hours, both Mrs. Bowden and Carmen moved together in the kitchen as if they were displaying a ballet piece in front of an auditorium full of people. Jade was the first one to show up to their house, and immediately went into helping Mrs. Bowden and Carmen with whatever they needed help with. In no time Mrs. Bowden had said that she needed to go to the grocery store to get an ingredient for one of her pies, and left. Carmen and Jade took that moment to take a break from cleaning the mess they had made.

Sitting at the kitchen table, Jade looked at Carmen and asked, "How are you?"

Carmen thought about that question before she responded. She said, "I've had a rough few days, but today I feel refreshed. It's been a long time since I felt this way."

Jade respected that Carmen told the truth. She nodded and said, "That's good. I know it's been hard but the absolute best thing in this situation is that you are here with us still. There will be some more rough patches but bear in mind that you have several best friends who want you to be at your best all the time. If you need us for anything, you better not ever hesitate."

Carmen exhaled and replied, "Jade, I would hate to be a burden on somebody. When Denise put me in this situation, you all put y'all lives on pause for a little while to make sure that I was good. I can't thank y'all enough for that."

"You were never a burden to any of us, so that thought doesn't even need to be in your head."

The room became silent as both women pondered on their short conversation. Carmen loved her best friends, but she didn't want them to have to cater to her every time she can't handle something. She was stronger than that, and needed to remind herself of that. Before she had thought of something to say, there was a knock on the door and she went up to go answer it. It was Amekia and Aziyah. They hugged each other until Carmen looked behind Amekia, and saw that Brandon was right behind her. Carmen stopped the hug, and looked at Amekia in confusion. Jade had walked up, noticing that Carmen was taking too long. She thought maybe Mrs. Bowden had returned from the store and needed help with the bags. She stopped in her steps in shock when she saw Brandon standing behind Amekia.

"Y'all could stop looking all stupid in the face. If y'all let us in, I could tell y'all that Brandon and I have made it official between us." Amekia dropped the bombshell with a nervous stance. Both Carmen and Jade looked at each other, trying to figure out when it had happened. *Thank God Sasha not coming,* Carmen thought, as she stepped out of Amekia and Brandon's way.

"Um, I—What?" Carmen said with her hands on her hips. As Amekia sat on the couch with Aziyah in her car seat in front of the couch, she laughed at Carmen's confusion. Brandon unpacked a *Pack N' Play,* and set it up in the living room. When he had it set up, Amekia laid Aziyah inside while Brandon made himself comfortable on the couch.

"Come on. Let's go in the kitchen while she is still napping," Amekia suggested, and headed towards the kitchen. Carmen and Jade couldn't help but eye each other in confusion before following Amekia into the kitchen. Once there, they all took a seat at the table.

Carmen began, "Um, what the fuck is going on?"

Amekia smirked as she began to explain. "There isn't really much to explain. Both Brandon and I came to the agreement to work on a relationship. Nothing more, nothing less."

Jade looked on, stunned. She couldn't begin to process what she just heard. She knew she had been spending time with Timothy, but she felt like she walked into a Twilight Zone. Jade asked, "You do know that he is still married to Sasha, right?"

"Yes, I know. We aren't rushing to get married. Shit, truth be told, I don't want to be married. Brandon and I are doing what we feel like is best for us. I never thought that I would actually be in a relationship with him, but why not? He came to me and told me his feelings, and I was tired of hiding behind mine."

"But—" Carmen began, but Amekia cut her off.

"There are no buts. This is the way it's going to be, so please try to get used to it. Y'all already know the man and all I'm asking is to treat him how y'all was before everything went down. Right now it's awkward but please don't make it more awkward." Amekia knew how sticky the situation could get, so she was hoping that her friends could try to be more receptive to them being together.

"Okay," both Carmen and Jade said in unison. Having got the elephant out of the room, the women decided to change the subject, but Mrs. Bowden came inside of the house and kicked them out of the kitchen, so she could finish her pie. When it was time to eat, the three women set the dining room table. The doorbell went off, causing everyone to stop. They knew Sasha wasn't coming, so they were clueless as to who could be at the door. Jade was the only one who knew. She invited Timothy. He didn't have any plans for Thanksgiving, due to his parents being gone, and he was an only child. Timothy didn't fuck with many of his cousins, and decided to stay in New York for the holiday. Jade walked away from everybody, and went to let Timothy in.

As Jade and Timothy made their way into the dining room, she began the introductions. "Everybody, this is Timothy. Timothy, this is Carmen and her mom Mrs. Bowden, Amekia, Brandon, and baby Aziyah." Everybody waved and smiled a hello to Timothy.

"I done slipped into a coma and this bitch went and got herself a man. Thank you, Father!" Carmen shouted, causing everybody to laugh. Timothy eased his way in, and started a conversation with everybody, easing Jade's mind about him fitting in. Dinner was going well, until the doorbell rang again. This time everybody held their breath because they just knew Sasha changed her mind. Amekia went to go open the door. When she came back to the dining room, she looked between Carmen and Mrs. Bowden.

Carmen's heart dropped to the pits of her stomach as she spoke. She said, "What, Amekia? What's going on?"

Still looking between mother and daughter, Amekia replied, "That's what I'm trying to figure out. There is this fine ass man at the door saying that Mrs. Bowden invited him over."

"Oh child, that's just my baby daddy, Carmen's real daddy," Mrs. Bowden replied, causing Jade and Amekia to break out in laughter.

Amekia said, "Mrs. Bowden, that man out there is too young to be Carmen's daddy."

Carmen's face was etched with embarrassment, and she looked at her mother. "Mama, no, you didn't invite Zaquan."

"I did. It's cold outside. Go let my baby father in. And Amekia, you better apologize to my man for keeping him waiting." Mrs. Bowden sounded serious. The room was silent until Jade and Amekia started laughing again. Brandon and Timothy looked on in confusion, as Carmen walked inside the dining room with a young dude.

"Everybody, this is my nurse—Zaquan. Zaquan, this is everybody and my mama." Carmen rolled her eyes. Jade and Amekia giggled like teenagers at the look that Carmen had on her face. It was a mixture of humiliation and embarrassment. Zaquan didn't look too comfortable either, until the conversation picked back up, then the men talked with the men while the women conversed with one another. Interrupting dinner again was the doorbell.

"Don't nobody come to this house any other day of the week, and now everybody wants to show up." Mrs. Bowden huffed as she got up from her seat and made her way to the door. Conversation resumed when the room knew that Mrs.

Bowden was coming back with people. Carmen hoped like hell that her sister and her boyfriend decided to join them after all. The room got silent when Sasha waltzed in with her girls and a man behind them.

"Daddy!" The girls ran over to Brandon and hugged him. They spoke to everybody in the room and immediately went to Amekia who was holding their sister.

Alexis looked up at Amekia and said, "Auntie Mekia, can we play with our sister?"

"Of course, sweetheart. Let me put her inside of her playpen." Amekia responded sweetly.

"Before y'all touch the baby, go wash y'all hands," Sasha said with authority in her voice. The room remained quiet until all of the kids were in the living room. The tension was so thick that both Timothy and Zaquan felt it but didn't want to speak on it. It wasn't their place, and they were leaving it to the parties that were involved. Mrs. Bowden felt the tension, and decided to leave the room to go watch over the kids.

With a smile on her face, Sasha began, "Nas, this is Carmen, Jade, and Timothy. Y'all this is Nas."

Nas looked over at Amekia, who was now wearing a scowl on her face. He said, "Sis."

Amekia glared at him and responded, "Bro."

Carmen slapped the tips of her fingers on the table in confusion. She put her fingertips to her temple and lightly rubbed, trying to figure everything the fuck out. She said, "Wait a goddamn minute. What in the actual fuck is going on here? Y'all are related?" Both Nas and Amekia nodded. Pointing towards Sasha and Nas, Carmen continued, "And y'all together?"

"Yes, Carmen," Sasha replied. She was the only one that seemed like she was comfortable in the situation.

"Well, isn't this the most awkward I've ever felt!" Carmen stated, speaking for almost everyone in the room. Everybody in the room had to admit, Carmen was right. Nevertheless, they sat at the table, picking imaginary lint from their clothes. This had nothing to do with Carmen and how the tension was so thick in the room, and she decided not to speak on it. Carmen eyed Amekia, who looked back at Carmen with a don't-start-with-me look on her face.

Sasha was getting tired of everybody acting like they couldn't feel the tension in the room. This was the first time in a long while that both Sasha, Amekia, and Brandon were in the same room, somewhat being civil to each other. And by being civil, that meant not speaking to one another. Sasha smirked and leaned back in her char, raising her left arm to rest it against the top of the chair. She said, "Let's not all talk at once. We know we can cut the tension with a knife, so how about we address the elephant in the room, shall we, Amekia?"

Carmen and Jade rolled their eyes while Brandon ran his hand down his face, and Nas just sat there as still as a statue. Amekia sat forward in her seat and calmly asked, "Was that a shot at my weight? Are you calling me fat? Are you trying to make me feel insecure and body-shame me because I fucked your nigga so good, he left your dumb ass alone? Hmm, is that it? 'Cause a thickums took your nigga?"

The way Amekia spoke let everyone in the room know she was taunting Sasha. If one looked into the situation, one might say that Sasha deserved it because she started the heat. Sasha knew she was being messy; the smirk that she displayed on her face said that she came to be petty. Brandon, seeing where this was going to go, and trying to nip it in the bud, said, "Now is not the not time. Not only do we have company around but we are also in someone else's house. Can we please have some respect for Mrs. Bowden?"

Brandon pleaded and Nas nodded in agreement. Carmen and Jade agreed. If Jade would have known that shit was going to go down like this, she wouldn't have invited Timothy over. Timothy didn't care what went down. At the end of the day, Jade's people were cool but he was there for her solely. He placed his hand on her thigh, just above her knee, and squeezed slightly, comforting Jade.

Amekia shook her head. "Nah, bitch had something to say. I was sitting here minding my business and I was going to keep doing so until this bitch said something to me." She was still calm, and that's what Carmen feared. If she knew her friend, shit was about to turn upside down fast, and she didn't want that to happen. This wasn't her crib, and she respected her mother's space. She wasn't about to allow these two heffas to tear her mother's shit up.

"That's not my fault, that's how you took it. I was just simply saying that let's address things and when I called your name, you took it upon yourself to get in your feelings. I wasn't calling you fat." Sasha responded with a chuckle.

"Nasir, you better put a muzzle on your bitch. Obviously, she ain't learning that I can and will dog-walk her bald-headed ass wherever, whenever." Amekia responded with a straight face.

"Come on, y'all. This beef should have been dead." Jade interrupted in exasperation, looking at Amekia.

"Whenever y'all say shit like that, y'all immediately look my way like I'm the one who is causing the issues. I ain't said boo to the bitch, and whether she intended to sneak diss me or not, bitch ain't got shit to say to me. I agreed to tolerate being around her, not getting attacked physically or verbally every single time we were in each other's presence."

Amekia's voice was rising, and they knew soon, Amekia was going to blow her top.

"Am I getting under your skin, Amekia?" Sasha taunted. Nas turned to look at Sasha.

In a stern voice, Nas began, "Yo, Sasha, what you doing ain't even called for. You see Mekia trying to be cool and you keep going. What you said earlier about the elephant in the room was uncalled for."

"That's not even how I meant it. It's not my fault her dumb ass took it that way." Sasha knew she meant it that way, Amekia did too. She was the queen of shade, and Amekia knew shade when it was being thrown. The room was silent again. No one moved in fear that it was going to cause another outburst from the two women.

Amekia got tired of the silence and was ready to go. She turned to Brandon and asked, "Babe, can you get Aziyah ready? I'm ready to go."

Brandon nodded as Sasha grunted. Jade spoke up, "Don't leave, Amekia."

"Nah, ole girl over here got so much to say and one thing I'm not finna do is fall into that and fight this bitch in front of the kids. Besides, I got enough respect for Mrs. Bowden to get the fuck up and leave so I'm not tearing her shit up."

Jade loved that Amekia was showing displays of growth.

Standing, Sasha said, "Bitch, we could go the fuck outside. 'Cause it seems like every time we fight, your ass got me from behind. Weak ass bitch!" Nas grabbed Sasha's wrist and tried to pull her down from the seat. He didn't understand what she wanted to fight Amekia for if she was there with him. If she agreed to be his girl, what could be the reason she wanted to fight Amekia for words that were exchanged and she knew she started it!

Amekia placed her hair in a ponytail and said, “You ain’t said nothing but a word. I'm still beating your ass.”

Carmen jumped in to try to stop the inevitable. She said, “Come on, y'all just stop. Y'all not tired of doing this shit every time y’all see each other.”

“Carmen, your friend invited me to a good time so I’m gonna enjoy it. I tried to fucking leave but she called me out like I’m a fucking pussy.” Amekia was getting riled up. Brandon had gotten up and tried to get Amekia to walk into the living room in order to leave. She was fighting against him. Zaquan and Timothy looked on quietly. This wasn’t their beef. Sasha walked on the opposite side of the table and headed to the back door through the kitchen. When Jade and Carmen realized that neither woman was gonna let the shit go, they followed behind Sasha. Brandon was still trying to get Amekia to walk away, but her mind was set. Sasha wanted a fight; that’s what was going to happen. She claimed that Amekia attacked her from behind, but Amekia was determined to show her that she could still whip her ass.

They all walked out of the house into the backyard. The sun had long gone down, and the air was slightly cold. The weather was being weird and, on that day, it felt like a spring night. Sasha was standing in the yard, waiting for Amekia to come out. This was the last fight that she was going to participate in. After this, she vowed to dead the situation. The only reason she wanted to fight was because she felt like every time they fought, Amekia sneaked up on her. She never had a fair advantage. Carmen and Jade walked up to Sasha, and tried to talk her out of the fight. Sasha’s defense was that she wanted a fair fight once and for all. Both Carmen and Jade thought the idea was ridiculous. They knew Amekia was going to kick Sasha’s ass again, and were only trying to save Sasha the embarrassment.

"Sasha, you are the more level-headed one out of all of us, why are you doing this?" Carmen tried to reason.

"Because of her mouth, Carmen," Sasha stated calmly.

Folding her arms across her chest, Carmen said: "But you started, Sasha, and you know you did. You did that shit on purpose. I thought you weren't even coming."

"Trust me, I didn't come to start shit with that bitch. Nas wanted to come so that he could spend the holiday with his sister. Maybe what I said was fucked up, but I don't give a fuck."

Jade interrupted and said, "She was walking away, Sasha. You the level-headed one but sometimes I fucking wonder where the fuck your head be. You had the opportunity to let this shit be, but instead you egged the shit on and you 'bout to get your ass whipped yet again!" Jade yelled. She was at her breaking point with this drama. Her two friends shared the same man as father to their children, and the kids were the ones that mattered in this situation. Jade gave props to Amekia. She was willing to walk away, and it was Sasha who was the one who pumped it up.

Amekia walked out of the house with Brandon following behind her. Her shoes were off, and she was coming toward Sasha like a train. When Amekia was close, Sasha got into a fighting stance, holding her arms up to block her face. Amekia walked up, and got into her fighting stance as well. The moment was intense, and the girls began yelling at each other. Getting tired of hearing Sasha run her mouth, Amekia planted her feet and faked swinging her left fist to Sasha's body, causing Sasha to drop her hands from her face, leaving it wide open. Placing all her weight behind this punch, Amekia cocked her right arm back, and jabbed Sasha in the face as hard and fast as she could. The hit landed on Sasha's nose, causing a flood of blood to leak from her nose. Sasha swiped at her nose, and rage gripped her body. She ran towards Amekia with her fists up and began swinging. The blows that Sasha landed did nothing but fire up Amekia's anger.

Carmen and Jade allowed the women to fight for a little while before they tried to break up the fight. With the way Amekia was jabbing and right-crossing Sasha, one who didn't know her would think she was a boxer. Sasha couldn't stay up on her feet, and ended up slipping on the misted over grass. When she fell to the ground, Amekia jumped on top of her and pummeled her fist into Sasha's face. When the men saw that Jade and Carmen were having a rough time stopping the fight, they stepped in.

"Who snuck who, hoe!" Amekia yelled with her hair wild on her head. She was livid. She was trying to fight out of Brandon's arms to get to Sasha. Sasha was trying to get up, but couldn't stay stable enough to do so. Carmen walked over to help Sasha up, all the while shaking her head.

"Y'all just be doing too damn much! Not every time y'all see each other, y'all gotta fight. Both of y'all bitches got children with the same nigga and they the ones who y'all should be worried about! Niggas can't even sit in the same room and be fucking cordial! Carmen, this is too much for me, I gotta go." Jade yelled. She felt like she was stuck in a bad episode of *Bad Girls Club*. Jade stormed off to the house with Timothy following close behind. Nothing more was said as Sasha and Nas walked towards the house. Zaquan and Brandon followed soon after Carmen asked them to give her and Amekia some time.

"Carmen, I was trying to walk away. Why did she have to push me?" Amekia stated. She had tears in her eyes, not for no other reason than her being pissed off to the max.

"I know, Amekia, and I'm sorry for that. I didn't know that she was coming. I asked her earlier and she told me that she wasn't." Carmen was pissed off too. Sasha was wrong, and Carmen couldn't wait for the next day so that she could speak with Sasha about it.

"You don't have to apologize for that gutter hoe! She is the one who needs to be apologizing. She is trying to make it seem like I didn't fight her without sneaking her and I'm tired of her bullshit. I wasn't going to say anything to her but she had to go and bother me!"

"I know, Amekia, and you better believe that I will be talking with Sasha tomorrow. Let's just call it a night. This has been too much." Carmen was over the situation, and she wanted everybody to leave so she could help her mother clean up the house and retreat to her bedroom to pop some percs and relax.

Chapter Twelve

Jade was pissed beyond measure. It had been a long time since they had all been in a room together because of Carmen being in the hospital. Jade had hoped they both Sasha and Amekia would be able to sit in the same room together. They were both grown ass women, and they needed to act like it. The ride back to Timothy's house was quiet. Timothy didn't like drama, and preferred to stay out of it. Just like most men, and Jade was thankful for that. Jade was so stuck in her own thoughts, she didn't realize that they arrived at Timothy's house. Timothy got out of the car and went to Jade's side to open the door for her. Before he allowed her to go up to the door, he wrapped his arms around her, instantly bringing her comfort.

Ever since the night Jade and Timothy had gone on a date, they have been inseparable. After the shit she went through with Darion, she was skeptical about being with another man ever again. The way Timothy stood up for her when Darion was attempting to rape her, and how he stayed by her side to support her, told her that she should give him a try. She liked the fact that he wasn't trying too hard to get with her. The way things flowed between them felt natural and unforced. That's what she had been looking for and when she would think about it, it upset her that she had to deal with Darion and contracted HIV.

On a cool October night, Timothy had cooked dinner for her and himself. He wanted to surprise her after she had a long day at work. When he opened the door for her, she stood there looking like the goddess that she was. She wore a yellow, short-sleeved strap dress that had a plunging neckline and a slit that reached her mid-thigh. She had on a pair of simple six-inch white pumps that made Timothy's dick rise to the occasion. The color of her dress looked so damn good against her chocolate-colored skin. Her hair hung down her back in her signature hairstyle of twists. Her lips shone from the gloss that she applied, and her eyes twinkled under the moonlight when she would look up at him. The smile he displayed on his face let Jade know that he was happy to see her.

"Well, are you going to let me in?" Jade asked, returning his smile.

"Oh, my bad. I was caught up in the brightness of your smile." Timothy replied with smoothness dripping from his mouth.

"Mmhm, I'm sure you were."

Jade entered the house, and immediately went to pour herself a drink. The week had been hell for her, and all she wanted was to enjoy a calm relaxing night with Timothy. At this point, they hadn't had sex. The sexual tension between them was evident, but something in Jade always stopped her from jumping on Timothy's dick. She didn't know his views on having sex with her because she was HIV positive. She was too embarrassed to even bring it up, so she left it alone.

"You ready?" Timothy asked.

"Ready? Ready for what?" Jade asked looking at Timothy like he had lost his mind.

With a chuckle and a shake of his head, Timothy took her hand into his and walked upstairs, through his bedroom, and onto the patio that was attached to his floor-to-ceiling windows. Outside, on the ground, there was a white and greyish silky sheep's skin run with a cushioning pad underneath laid out. On top of the rug there was a long wooden platter that held two plates of food. On the plates were a mixture of roasted baby finger carrots, small red potatoes, cauliflower, and Brussel sprouts; rice pilaf with braised lamb shanks were next to the vegetables. A metal bucket sat with ice inside, and a bottle of Moët was chilling on top of the ice. There were pillows surrounding the rug, serving its purpose for comfort. Jade's mouth seemed like it didn't want to close, as she looked at the sight before her.

"Timothy, what is this?" she asked.

"I wanted you to enjoy a night of relaxation. You told me you had a rough week and today was the worst. I just want you to relax."

"Aww. Thank you, I appreciate it." Jade turned around, wrapped her arms around him, and placed a kiss on his lips. Jade took her feet out of shoes, and got comfortable on the rug. Timothy joined her, and they sat there and ate. Timothy brought the dinnerware to the kitchen when they were done, and placed them inside of the dishwasher. When he was done, he went back to join Jade on the rug. The cool breeze was refreshing for them as they sipped on the champagne. Soon enough, the conversation led to Jade being curious and wanting to know how he felt about having sex with someone he knows is HIV positive.

"It took you forever to ask me." Timothy chuckled. He continued, "I am very well-educated on sex with a person who is positive. My cousin was diagnosed with HIV, and my auntie told me that I needed to educate myself. I was afraid of contacting the virus by cross contamination, and my auntie pulled me to the side and told me that I needed to really educate myself because I was making my cousin feel a certain way. I would go in the bathroom after him with a bottle of bleach and clean everything down before I used it. Even if I didn't use it, I thought I was being helpful to everybody else. When my auntie told me how I was making my cousin feel, I did just what she suggested and did my research. While I don't make it business going around

having sex with HIV positive women, I do know how to protect myself and the woman I am having sex with. Even if I didn't know that a woman was positive, I still made sure that I followed the same precautions on non-positive women."

"So if you know what you got to do to protect yourself, why haven't you tried to have sex with me?" Jade asked. She was beginning to feel like Timothy didn't look at her in a sexual manner because there couldn't be any other reason as to why he hadn't tried her yet.

"Because I like you, Jade. And when I like someone, sex isn't the first thing I'm trying to get. I want to know you for you and not what your insides feel like. If sex was the case, then I would just be slinging dick to any woman that came my way. I'm different and a nigga like me is rare. Shit, there are women willing to give it up to me in the first hour of meeting a nigga. At this point in my life, I'm looking for a woman to settle down with. To share my wealth with. It gets lonely sometimes."

Jade looked at him with lust in her eyes. He was right, he was different and rare. She looked up at Timothy and said, "What about children?"

"I want those too."

"Well, how will that happen? If we are together when the time comes that you want children, how will that happen?"

"There are different options. I can ejaculate in a cup and they can put it in you. Simple as that."

When Jade found out she was HIV positive, she thought about her chance at having kids, and immediately decided that she wouldn't have kids. She didn't want to run the risk of passing this deadly virus to her child. It was her stupid mistake for having unprotected sex with a nigga that she barely knew. Jade looked down at her hands and whispered, "I don't want children."

"If you didn't want children, why ask?" Timothy asked in confusion.

"I don't want to pass this virus to my children. I just wouldn't be able to live with myself if I passed it to them."

Timothy got quiet and understood where she was coming from. He moved closer to Jade and wrapped his arms around her from behind. She leaned against him, as tears threatened to spill from her eyes. Throughout that night, Timothy held Jade. The next morning, Timothy asked Jade if she had a second opinion about her test results. There was something sitting on his heart, and he wanted her to get a second opinion. Jade wasn't too eager to go and get tested again. She knew she was positive, and she didn't want to relive another doctor telling her that she was positive.

The fight between Jade's friends had her exhausted. Timothy helped Jade inside his house in silence. Jade had been spending a large amount of time at Timothy's house, but at that moment she just wanted to be alone. She knew that Timothy just wanted to make sure she was good, but she wanted to deal with the heartbreak of their sisterhood alone. Instead of jumping in the shower before she went to bed, she went to sleep without doing so.

***

"Girls, go shower and get in the bed!" Sasha yelled when they entered the house. She was furious, and she couldn't blame anybody except herself. She had gotten beat up once again, and she was embarrassed. She not only got beat up in front of Carmen, Jade, and Brandon; but also two new faces and her man. Sasha couldn't lie, Amekia fucked her up. While the girls ran upstairs to go shower, she went into the downstairs bathroom and looked at herself in the mirror. Her hair was all over her head, she had a knot on her right eyebrow, her left eye was swollen and beginning to bruise. Her nose wasn't broken, but the dried-up blood that dripped from her nose to her lips made the damage look worse. The scratches that adorned her neck and chest were bright red and seeping droplets of blood. Before she washed her face, she grabbed a detangling brush from her vanity, and began to fix her hair. In the mirror, her eyes caught Nas leaning against the door frame of the bathroom, and she ended up rolling her eyes.

"If I would have known that's what you were going over there to do, I would have stopped you. I asked you before we left this house if you were gonna be on some bullshit and you told me no. Why would you lie?" Nas asked calmly.

Sasha sighed. The last thing she wanted was to hear his mouth about what happened. She said, "That wasn't why I was going. I legit wanted to spend time with Jade and Carmen and when I saw her face it reminded me of everything that had gone down."

"And you feel good about what happened? Because if you are, you should rethink that. You look like a hot ass mess and you looked like even a bigger one when Amekia was trying to walk away. You had your daughters crying on the way here because they wanted to know why you looked the way you did."

When her hair was detangled, she placed it in a ponytail, all the while rolling her eyes. She responded, "I forgot you're team Amekia."

"I'm team right and you were wrong, Sasha. You didn't have to address nothing. Niggas is moving on from the situation and you just had to make it worse. Look at your face. If she beat your ass twice before, why try for a third?"

"Third time's a charm," Sasha said.

"Are you serious? You got your ass handed to you. If she did you dirty the first two times, what makes you think she wouldn't do it again?"

Sasha wasn't in the mood to hear his scolding. She wasn't a child. Running water over a fresh wash rag, she lathered the rag with *Dial* antibacterial soap and began to clean her face. Her face was in so much pain, that she barely got the blood off her face as she washed it. She didn't bother to respond to Nasir. She needed to ice her face to get the swelling down. She was returning back to work that Monday, and wanted to at least have the swelling down. The make-up would cover up the bruises. When she was done in the bathroom, she made her way into the kitchen to make a drink for herself. Nas was following her around, expecting her to reply to his answer. He was going to be waiting forever because Sasha had no plans in replying.

"You just gonna walk around here and choose not to answer me, Sasha? You are a grown ass woman and instead of ignoring me, you could tell me that you don't want to talk about it." Nas watched her grab her cup of *D'usse* and a zip lock bag full of ice into the living room. She sat on the couch and turned the TV on.

"Nas, I don't want to talk about it." She sighed.

"That's all you had to say from the beginning," Nas said. He took a seat next to her on the couch, and took the zip lock out of her hands. Before she began to complain, he placed the zip lock bag over her knot and eye. In silence, they watched TV and tried to enjoy the rest of their Thanksgiving.

***

It took Carmen two hours to put food away and clean up the kitchen before she was able to relax. Surprisingly, her mother was still up and watching TV in the living room. Carmen exhaled as she turned the kitchen light off, and went to join her mother.

"Mama, I'm sorry about tonight. I really didn't know that Sasha was going to show up." Carmen apologized because the last thing she wanted to do was, ruin her mother's Thanksgiving. Her mother was finally having a house full of people and was excited about the holiday, and it was ruined because of the drama between her friends. She was too embarrassed to say the least.

"Girl, that was the most excitement that I have seen in a long time. A little bit of drama won't hurt nobody." Mrs. Bowden's reply caused Carmen to laugh.

"Well, I take my apology back. However, I would like to know what possessed you to invite Zaquan?"

"You know he my baby daddy." Mrs. Bowden chuckled. She continued, "I thought that there could have been something between you and him and wanted you two to bond over dinner. From what I saw tonight, you were all over him, skinning and grinning all in his face and then Sasha and her drama showed up. I think that if she didn't, y'all would be upstairs fucking like rabbits."

Carmen leaned back onto the couch while holding her stomach, laughing. When she caught her breath, she said, "Mama, ain't you filled with the Holy Spirit? Why are you cussing like that?"

"I've said this once before and I will say it again, the Lord knows my heart. He made me the way I am so he knows what he signed up for. I'm Holy but try me and I'm knucking and bucking and ready to fight."

"Mama! Where did you learn that saying?" Carmen asked. She was shocked her mother was using such "hip" terms.

Mrs. Bowden waved her hand at Carmen and said, "Girl, that book face app that all y'all young folks are using."

Carmen slid off the couch like New York's mother did in *Flavor of Love,* and burst into hysterical laughter. Wiping tears from her eyes, she said, "Oh my God, Mama! It's Facebook!"

"You know just what the hell I meant. My point is, you can be Holy and still defend yourself when it calls for you to do so."

Carmen couldn't stop herself from laughing. She enjoyed this side of her mother. When she was in one of her holier-than-thou moments, she could be a tad annoying by constantly quoting bible scriptures and speaking in tongues, so this side of her mom she truly enjoyed. Carmen chilled with her mother for another half an hour before she decided to head upstairs. The percocets were calling her name all day, and she couldn't wait to indulge.

***

Amekia and Brandon arrived home a little after ten o'clock. When they left Carmen's, it was close to nine and Amekia needed a drink. Brandon pulled up to the liquor store and grabbed a bottle of strawberry watermelon Malibu. It wasn't strong, and was perfect for Amekia to get a buzz. When they left the liquor store, Amekia asked Brandon if he could park by the Mohawk River before they went home. He did what she asked, but that was only because Aziyah was already asleep.

"I'm sorry that Sasha keeps antagonizing you. I don't know what I could do in order for this shit to stop." Brandon apologized as soon as he put the car in park.

Amekia placed the bottle to her lips, and took a nice long sip. When she pulled the bottle from her lips, she shook her head. She replied, "Brandon, there ain't nothing in this world gonna stop that woman. If she feels like attacking me, she's gonna do so. That was the third time she decided to run up on me. I'ma give her this work every time she runs up because that is exactly what she is looking for."

"You would think that since Nas came over confessing that they were together, then she would be on her best behavior."

"Ha! How long have you been married to her and you still don't know how she is? Man, were you absent for your whole marriage?" Amekia chuckled, taking another swig from the bottle.

"I was. I mean, things weren't all bad but that shit wasn't all good either. I love my baby girls, but sometimes I do wonder how it would have been if I had them with somebody else."

This wasn't the chance for Amekia to bash Sasha. She loved Alexis and Aliana as nieces, and she refused to partake in anything negative towards them. Amekia understood where Brandon was coming from. Sasha wasn't a deadbeat mom, but she wasn't the best either. So many women wished that they had baby fathers that took care of their responsibilities. Hell, it was hard for women just to have the fathers in their kids' lives. Brandon was there and very active, and Amekia could foresee what a disaster their divorce could be.

With a serious tone, Amekia said: "I just want all of this to end. I say I want to beat Sasha ass every time she decides she wants to feel froggy, but the reality is that it's gonna get old and I want it nipped in the bud now."

"Let's give it a few days to cool things down and I will go have a talk with her."

"Maybe I will go with you."

Brandon shook his head. He knew that wouldn't be a good idea because they could yet again break out in a brawl. He said, "I don't think that would be a good idea, Amekia."

"And why not?"

"Sasha is a smart woman and she's gonna think it's a set-up. Let me talk with her alone. I'm not even gonna go over to the house. I will ask her to meet me somewhere to discuss the terms of our divorce and then lead into the conversation what happened between y'all. One thing is for certain, this shit needs to stop."

"I agree. Come on, we can head home now. I'm tired and need a shower."

Brandon turned the car on and headed home. The situation between Amekia and Sasha was weighing heavy on his mind even before the fight. He was the primary cause of this situation. In order for him and Amekia to move on and live peacefully, he would have to make sure they don't end up killing each other whenever they were in each other's presence.

Chapter Thirteen

Jade walked into her house after a long day of work. She had been going to Timothy's house after work for weeks, only stopping at her house to grab clothes. Most of her clothes had piled up at Timothy's house. Ever since she had been staying there, she would come every week, on a Wednesday, to come clean. It had been a week since Sasha and Amekia fought at Carmen's, and she hadn't spoken to either one. Both Sasha and Amekia called and texted her non-stop, and she never answered or responded to the texts. She was upset with them fighting like they did. She vowed that she wasn't speaking to them until they had gotten their shit together.

When Jade walked into her house, she dropped her work bag at the door, and headed straight to her room to change into some workout clothes. Walking back into the living room, she turned some music on and began to clean her house from top to bottom. She did more singing and dancing than she did cleaning, but she managed to get it done. Two hours later, she was done and had worked up a sweat. She couldn't wait until she got to Timothy's to take a shower. Jade turned the music off, went into her room, and began to gather her things from her room. Then she headed back to the front door. Grabbing her work bag, she put her keys in her hand and opened her door. On the opposite side, there stood Denise. Her hand was raised as if she was about to knock on the door.

Jade looked at Denise with a scowl. "Bitch, you got some nerve showing your face at my door. Are you stupid? Or are you dumb? 'Cause, bitch, I think you both." Jade put her bag down.

"Wait, Jade. I need to speak with you. I know who set Carmen's house on fire." Denise was nervous that Jade was about to fold her up like a folding chair.

"Excuse me? If you know then what the fuck are you doing here? You need to be at the police station." Jade sassed and folded her arms across her chest.

"I'm scared to go. I don't want them to think I had anything to do with it because I know."

"Bitch, you giving me weird vibes. You should have said something about knowing who it was."

Denise sighed and looked at Jade. She tried to make her face look serious as she said, "I'm sure that Carmen told you about why we broke up. Well, the dude Bilal was mad that she turned him down and didn't want to be in a three-way relationship with us. He was furious to the point where he was obsessed with talking about her. He started to follow her and when he saw her alone, he figured that he would start a fire, just to scare her. But the fire got out of control and she ended up almost dying."

"If you knew all of this, why didn't you say so long ago? This isn't making sense to me. You were in a relationship with Carmen and you didn't know how she was as a person? You hurt her, and her being caught in a house fire that she barely made it out of somehow ended up being her fault. Like this the weirdo shit that I absolutely cannot deal with. Take your information to the cops so that I know that it was real. Until then, bitch, you still a suspect. Now get off my porch before I beat the shit out of you." Jade was furious. It was almost four months since Carmen had been in the house fire. For Denise to approach her at her house and blame Bilal was weird to her.

"Please, Jade." The desperation in her tone caused Jade to pause just for a second. She looked at Denise and saw the pitiful look in her eyes.

"Let me ask you something. Why didn't you just go to the police when you found out it was Bilal? Why did you let four months go past before saying anything?" Jade needed to know why Denise had a change of heart. Something was fishy, and Jade didn't like it one bit.

Denise looked away as she thought about if she wanted to tell Jade the truth or not. She placed her nails in her mouth, and bit on them nervously. Jade was getting ready to walk away because of Denise not talking. Denise saw this, and she quickly opened her mouth. She said, "I was scared to tell y'all. Bilal told me that if I said anything, he was going to make sure that I wouldn't see the light of day. I didn't know what to do."

"So why now?" Jade wanted to know.

"Because I still love her, Jade. The way things ended was fucked up but I loved the fuck out of Carmen."

Jade still wasn't moved. There was something that was telling her that Denise wasn't telling the truth. Jade picked up her bag again, walked out of the door fully, locked her door and walked away. She was going to have to speak to Sasha even though she wasn't feeling her at that moment. Jade was in a pretty much good mood before she saw Denise, and she wanted to stay that way. Timothy always wanted her at her best, and that's what she wouldn't give to Denise. Jade walked to her car and drove off after she picked the perfect song to listen to.

Timothy was chilling in the living room when she walked into the house. Jade called ahead to get Timothy to unlock the door, and he did just that. His heart felt like it skipped a beat when he saw Jade enter the living room. She slid into his lap, happy to see him.

"Phew! You didn't think to shower before you decided to bring your ass over here?" Timothy asked, clinching his nose. Jade wasn't expecting him to say that to her, and her mouth dropped open in shock. While Timothy thought what he said was the funniest thing in the world, Jade sat up in Timothy's lap and raised her arms to get a whiff. She didn't smell anything from her underarms. She then cocked her legs open and used her hand to fan herself to see if he could smell her pussy. There was nothing there either. She looked back at Timothy who was still cackling.

"I don't stink!" she yelled. Getting up from his lap, she ran off to his bathroom to take a shower. While she was washing up, she laughed good and hard as she recalled how she was trying to smell herself. Her irritation with that childish comment from Timothy disappeared as she washed her body. When she was done, she wrapped a towel around her body, and went inside of Timothy's bedroom. He was in there laying in bed with the remote in his hands, searching to find something for them to watch. Using the towel, she patted herself dry and applied African shea butter all over her body. She could feel Timothy's eyes on her body, but she didn't acknowledge him. They had yet to have sex, and Jade was starting to feel like they wouldn't unless she was the one who initiated it. Jade never had a problem before initiating sex, but her situation had changed and she was a nervous wreck thinking about it.

Interrupting Jade's thoughts, Timothy said, "I took it upon myself to schedule both of us an appointment with my doctor. I don't want you to think that I'm trying to control the situation but I just want you to get a second opinion. I decided to get checked out as well to make sure that you were comfortable." She appreciated his concern for her, but she wasn't in the business of wanting to hear that she was HIV positive again.

Jade sighed as she climbed into the bed with just her panties on. She replied, "I really appreciate your concerns when it comes to my health, but I don't know if you realize it would suck to hear that I am positive again."

Timothy stretched his arm out so that Jade could snuggle up under him like she liked to do. He asked, "You don't think that there could have been some type of mix-up? Like someone accidentally swapped the specimens?"

"Trust me, I thought that could have been a possibility, but the chances of me being misdiagnosed is highly unlikely. However, because you care so much about my health, I will go get retested. And when the test results come back, I would like to have very, very protected sex with you." Jade said the last part with a smirk on her face. Timothy couldn't hold his laughter in, and laughed just from the look on her face. He agreed with her, and they talked until they both fell asleep in each other's arms.

The next morning, Jade was sleeping soundly when Timothy walked in with a tray of food. On the tray was a small bowl of buttery grits with Cajun shrimp on top, fluffy eggs, beef bacon, and a glass of ice-cold orange juice. After he woke her up, Jade smiled and sat up in the bed. She was thankful that it was Saturday, and she didn't have to worry about rushing to get to school. Timothy placed the tray over her legs and placed a small kiss on her lips.

Jade smiled. "Thank you. You are so sweet."

"It's the least I can do before I drag you to this appointment."

"And that's what's making this day better already." Jade couldn't contain the smile on her face. This was the first time in a long time that she was this happy. If she had to admit it, she loved it. When she began to eat, Timothy got in the shower. He had already eaten, and wanted Jade to eat in peace. By the time he was done in the shower, Jade had finished eating and laid her outfit on the bed. The temperature had dropped significantly after Thanksgiving. Jade chose to wear a pair of fitted black Nike joggers, a white long-sleeved shirt and black and white Nike 95's. Walking into the bathroom, Jade looked at herself in the mirror and admired her glow. Thinking about how Timothy made her feel, she grinned. Shaking the nasty thoughts in her head free, she undressed and began the shower water. When the water was to her liking, she got in and washed her body twice with her favorite body wash.

"What time is the appointment again?" Jade asked, entering the room. Timothy caught her attention, and she couldn't stop herself from staring. He was wearing black distressed jeans, a white turtleneck, and wheat-colored Timbs. He was standing in front of his wall mirror, brushing his hair.

"Eleven-thirty." Timothy looked down at his watch, and realized they were running a little late. He continued, "I don't want to rush you but its ten forty-five already and it's going to take at least twenty minutes to get there."

"Okay, I got you. I won't even put my make-up on."

"You don't need it anyway. You're beautiful just the way you are." Timothy liked looking at Jade, whether she had make-up or not. He preferred her natural state, and he couldn't wait until she got that in her head. With a smile on her face, Jade quickly applied lotion to her body and got dressed. She let her twist hang down her back. Spritzing her favorite perfume, *Yellow Diamond* by Versace, she was ready to go. On the ride to the doctor's office, Timothy kept a conversation going to keep her mind off where they were going and why they were going. Little did Jade know that Timothy was nervous about going to the doctor. Before they met, he wasn't a saint and it had been a hot minute since he had gone to go get tested. He hid his nervousness well because Jade had never suspected a thing.

When they got to the office, they approached the front desk and checked in. The look of nervousness washed over Jade's face. Timothy picked her hand up in his and rubbed the back of her hand with his thumb, trying to comfort not only her but himself as well. The wait for the nurse to come and get them didn't take long. Timothy and Jade were separated and placed into different rooms, further causing them worry. Jade's nurse was very pleasant and attentive to her, telling her a story and why she was there. As soon as Jade was done giving this nurse an earful, the nurse began to check Jade's vitals. Leaving the room, the nurse told her that the doctor would be with her soon.

Jade looked around the room, trying to get her thoughts straight. Her hands were sweaty, and she had the impulse to move. She slid off the table, closed the gown tightly around her body, and paced the floor. Not knowing what else to do, she bowed her head and paced the floor. She began to pray. *Dear Lord, please give me the strength to get through this appointment. Please give me the strength to accept the second set of results. Please give me strength. Amen.* Jade wasn't big on prayer, so she always kept it short and simple. Lying back on the table, she closed her eyes and allowed a calming sense come over her body. Soon after, there was a knock on the door. In walked a short cute doctor dressed in powder blue pink scrubs and a white coat. The nervousness that Jade felt prior to the doctor entering the room was no longer there. Jade invited the doctor in the room with a warm smile.

The woman greeted Jade. "Hi, I'm Doctor Nash and you are?"

"Hello, I'm Jade. Jade Rios." Jade smiled, reaching her hand out to shake Dr. Nash's hand.

"Nice meeting you. Okay, let's jump right on in. What brings you here today?" Dr. Nash asked with a small smile on her face.

"If it wasn't for my boyfriend dragging me here, I wouldn't be. I genuinely appreciate his concerns for me but I've come to accept the life that I now have to live. Almost seven months ago, I went to my doctor because I wasn't feeling well. We did tests and the only thing that came back was a positive HIV test. Timothy wants me to get a second opinion and I can't quite tell you his reason as to why but I'm doing it for him. I have already accepted that I have this virus, but I do need help with how to take care of myself in order to live a long life. At least as long as this virus will allow me to live."

"Okay. That's a great thing that you have accepted it. I have many people who come in here who want me to run their blood samples four and five times. This office is the best in the city for what we do, and we only need to run the sample two times before we come and give the patient their results. Today we are going to give you a rapid swab test and also take some of your blood. Okay? The swab takes about twenty minutes to come back, and the blood sample results will be on our portal. When the nurse comes back in here to administer the tests, she will have some paperwork on the portal that lets you know how to create your account and your results will appear there. Okay?"

"Okay. Thank you." Jade responded. Dr. Nash asked her a few more questions before she was finished. Afterwards, the doctor left the room. Two minutes later, the nurse that was previously in there, walked in. She explained to Jade everything that was in the paperwork before she instructed Jade what to do while she was doing the swab test. Next was her blood being drawn. She wondered if Timothy was still in his room.

"All done," the nurse said.

"Oh, that was fast."

"I try to get patients in and out because I know how people can be when they go to the doctor. They think that they will receive the worst news possible and raise their blood pressure. But you were calm through and through." The nurse complimented Jade while placing a band aid over her arm.

"I was a nervous wreck when I walked in here, but a quick prayer to God got me all the way together." Jade laughed. Soon enough she walked out of the room. Jade got dressed and laid back on the table. Jade's phone dinged, signaling that she had a text message. She reached into her purse and got her phone. When she read the message displayed on the screen, she knew that she had to be seeing shit. She bypassed responding to the text message, and called Sasha.

"Hello," Sasha said, sounding like she was in tears.

"I just got your text message. Is it true?" Jade asked. The text was from Sasha. It stated that Denise had turned herself in, claiming she was the one who set Carmen's house on fire.

"Yes, it's true. I'm so mad. This whole time I knew she was behind it but I did nothing to bring her ass down."

"You did all that you could, Sasha. I want to know why she just turned herself in. She caught me coming out of my apartment and told me that it was all Bilal. She said that she wanted to tell but he threatened to kill her."

"Why didn't you tell me? I would have done something with that information."

"Because it just happened yesterday."

Sasha sighed. "I just told Carmen. She hasn't responded yet. I'm about to head down to the station to see if I can get any information. I will call you with an update."

"Okay. I'm texting Amekia now to let her know what's going on."

Sasha grunted as she said her goodbyes. Jade wasn't being insensitive about telling her she was texting Amekia. Jade felt like they needed to get over what they had going on. If they weren't going to talk to each other, they could at least resolve the issue and stop fighting each other when they were in each other's presence. After Jade texted Amekia what was going on, she placed her phone inside her purse. She was lost in thought when the nurse came back in with a smile on her face. Jade sat up and looked at the nurse. She didn't know if she had good news or if she was just being polite.

"Your swab results are back," the nurse said.

"Okay. Don't keep an asshole in suspense. I'm prepared for it." Jade looked sad.

"It came back negative."

Jade looked up from the floor to make sure she had heard the nurse correctly. She asked, "What? What do you mean they came back negative?"

"That's what it said. You don't seem happy about it."

"That's because I am confused. How did I test positive the first time and now I am negative? I don't understand."

Knock! Knock!

In walked Dr. Nash with a bright smile on her face. When she came in, she said: "I saw the results. I don't know how you had a positive, but the swab test is ninety-two percent accurate. That's a pretty high percentile. Of course, we want to wait until the blood test comes back but I know that's gonna be negative right along with the swab."

"Oh my God!" Jade shouted and slid to the floor. She clasped her hands together and thanked God. The amount of tears falling from her eyes was like a broken dam. Timothy knocked on the door before he walked in. When he saw Jade on her knees crying and Dr. Nash rubbing her back, he instantly felt horrible. He should have just listened when Jade was telling him not to go. He instantly dropped to the floor with Jade. She was saying something that he couldn't quite figure out. He wrapped his arms around her and began rocking her.

Speaking into the top of her head, Timothy said: "I'm sorry, babe. I should have listened to you when you said you didn't want to come. I'm so sorry."

"Unhand me, Timothy. My results were negative." Jade sniffled with a smile on her face.

"What? Are you sure?" he asked, looking up at Dr. Nash and the nurse.

"We are positive. Now I don't know how her previous doctor got the results wrong and you can sue for malpractice, but the current swab is ninety-two percent accurate. I told Jade here that I still want her to wait for the results of the blood test but I have no doubt that those will be negative too."

"So what the hell were you doing on the floor?" Timothy asked Jade.

"Because it was the only thing I could do in order to praise God. Now get off me so I can march down to my ex doctor's office to wreak havoc. Dr. Nash, if it's okay with you, I'd appreciate it if you take me on as a new client."

"Of course. There is necessary paperwork for you to fill out and you need to call your insurance to let them know what happened and that you are changing your primary care physician. I also think that you should hire a lawyer. There is no telling how many times that this has happened."

"Okay, thank you. You have no idea how grateful I am to you." Jade responded and pulled both Dr. Nash and the nurse into a hug.

Timothy cleared his throat and asked, "What about my results?"

"Oh, you're negative across the board." The nurse replied once Jade let them go.

Timothy pulled Jade into his arms and placed a kiss on her lips. He whispered only for Jade to hear, "Let's go home. I'm trying to rearrange some of your organs."

Jade couldn't help but laugh as she gathered her paperwork, and they left out hand in hand. This was the happiest day in Jade's life thus far, and she couldn't contain herself. She finally felt comfortable to have sex with Timothy, and she knew that it would be a while before either one of them would come up for air.

Chapter Fourteen

Things for Sasha and Nas were going pretty damn well. It had been two weeks since Denise confessed to setting Carmen's house on fire. Sasha had gotten a chance to speak with Denise, and she told her everything. She even confessed that Bilal had nothing to do with the fire. He, in fact, was out of town when she set the fire. She admitted that she wanted Sasha to join in on a relationship with her and Bilal. Carmen never told her friends that Denise brought this to her attention. She declined Denise, and that's how Denise decided to do what she did. She couldn't handle the rejection. She told the detectives that she had only wanted Carmen to be scared but the fire had gotten out of hand. She didn't mean for Carmen to get hurt. Sasha couldn't stay in the room long enough. She never understood how people couldn't handle rejection and instead of accepting it, they went and hurt the other party involved.

Christmas was coming around the corner, and Brandon had invited Sasha out so that she could help him with Christmas shopping for their girls. She wanted to decline, but Nas encouraged her to go. Nas loved spending time with her kids, and they enjoyed him too. He let them get away with shit that their mother wouldn't. For that reason alone, they loved him.

"Where y'all going shopping?" Nas asked when he walked into their bedroom. He had moved in a week after Thanksgiving. It was Sasha's idea and he wasn't going to turn it down. He lived in a one-bedroom apartment in a nice neighborhood, but if Sasha and the girls wanted to come over, he didn't have enough space for everybody.

"He said he wants to hit both Colonie and Crossgates Mall," Sasha said, placing her hair in a ponytail. She had been feeling under the weather, and didn't plan to dress up. She had on a pair of Nike sweatpants, a shirt, and a hoodie.

"Don't you look fashionable!" Nas joked as he looked down at her attire.

"Nas, you know I haven't been feeling well lately. And if it wasn't because we are shopping for the girls, I wouldn't have even gone."

"I know. You have been in a foul mood lately. If you are not having mood swings, you're eating and sleeping all the time. If I didn't know any better, I would think that you were pregnant." Nas chuckled. Sasha paused what she was doing and looked at Nas. Quickly, she thought back to when she last had her period, and gasped as she realized she hadn't gotten it since before Thanksgiving.

"I just thought I was stressed," Sasha said as she rushed to the bathroom and closed the door behind her. Nas was stuck in place, sitting on the bed. In the bathroom, Sasha reached under the bathroom sink and took a pregnancy test out. She thanked God that she had to pee. She sat down on the seat and opened her legs, placing the test under her and peed on the stick. She placed the stick on the countertop of the sink, wiped, and washed her hands. Her heart pounded in her chest. She didn't know how she would feel if she was pregnant. Her relationship with Nas was just showing progress, and she didn't know how he would feel if the test results were positive. She didn't even know how she would feel. Minutes ticked by, and she couldn't bring herself to look at the test. Nas was growing impatient and knocked on the bathroom door. Sasha opened the door and watched Nas' eyes zoom in on the test on the sink. He walked in and picked up the test.

"Yes!" Nas yelled excitedly. Sasha didn't know if he was happy that it was negative, so she peered over his shoulder and right in her face were two pink lines. Her heart sank. She didn't have to ask how he felt because he was still hooping and hollering while she was shedding tears. Nas placed his arms around Sasha. She needed to make an appointment asap to see how far along she was. She hoped that she wasn't that far along because that would mean that the baby was Nas'.

Sasha looked at the time and was grateful that she was running late. She didn't want to have this conversation right now with Nas. She said, "I have to get going. I'm running late."

"Are you not happy?" Nas asked, picking up on her somber tone.

"I am, babe. I'm just feeling a little nauseous."

"Maybe you should eat before you go."

"I will pick something up on the way. Don't let the girls run over you. I know how they look at you and you fell right into their trap." Sasha chuckled, trying to lighten her mood.

"That's because they know that I hate telling them no. I will have dinner on the table by the time you get back. What are you in the mood for?"

Sasha took some time to think about what she had wanted for dinner. Just the thought of food made her want to vomit. She replied, "As long as it's not pork. I thought I wanted smothered pork chops but just the thought got my stomach turning."

Nas laughed and replied, "Okay. I got you. Have fun shopping."

With that Nas placed a kiss on Sasha's lips and walked out of their bedroom, whistling happily. Pushing the positive test results to the back of her mind, she put her sneakers on. Before she left, she told her daughters to behave. On the ride over to Colonie Mall, Sasha passed by a Dunkin' Donuts store and purchased a cream cheese and everything bagel, together with a small iced latte. She was good and full when she got out of her car and walked to the entrance to meet Brandon at the food court.

"Hey there, baby daddy," Sasha said when she walked up on him.

"What's up, Sasha?" Brandon replied with a chuckle.

"You ready to spend some coins? 'Cause your daughters' lists are pretty long for Santa this year."

"Their lists are always long. They are truly their mother's daughters."

"Oh, shut up."

Brandon got up from his seat, and they began their walk to Macy's. They spent almost a thousand dollars on their daughters, and it was time for them to hit up Foot Locker for their footwear. Things were going good until they ended up at Crossgates Mall. Sasha had gotten hungry, and they decided to hit up the Wendy's in the food court. When they got their food, they searched for empty seats, but that was almost impossible. The mall was always so busy, and that was one of the reasons why she hated going to Crossgates.

"I've been meaning to call you and touch base with you on the specifics about our divorce," Brandon said after his first bite of his burger.

"What about it?" Sasha questioned.

"I was thinking that I could have the girls on weekends and a full month for the summer."

"Why only every weekend? I would like to do things with them too, Brandon."

"They live with you for the rest of the days of the week. I'm only asking for the weekends and not half the week."

"Half of the week would just be absurd, Brandon."

"Exactly. That's why I'm asking for the weekends."

Sasha sighed. She lost her appetite, and couldn't bring herself to agree. He knew that she hated doing things with the girls during the week, especially because school was around. She folded her arms across her chest and said, "Would it include every other weekend and all important holidays such as Christmas, Thanksgiving, and Easter?"

Brandon gave it some thought. He replied, "Okay I can deal with that."

"Anything else?"

"As a matter of yes. I'm willing to pay child support but the spousal support I can't jack."

Sasha looked at him like he lost his mind. She said, "Why can't you jack the spousal support? You don't think that I deserve that much from the shit I dealt with because of you and Amekia?"

"You have a damn good job, Sasha. You are the most sought out defense attorney in the Capital District. I'm sure you can take care of yourself and the girls. I'm only agreeing to the child support because they are my kids. And what happened with myself and Amekia ain't got shit to do with you asking for spousal support. You will not be using my money to add onto your money for you to spend on a grown ass man."

"Oh, okay. I see what the problem is. You think that I'm going to use that money to spend on Nas? You are a fucking trip. What I spend my money on and how I spend it shouldn't matter. I want spousal support. I'm already giving you the girls on the holidays."

Brandon eyed Sasha. He wanted her to hear him and hear him clear. He said, "I'm not paying spousal support. That's it and that's final."

"I deserve spousal support! You are really a character. I'm gonna fight for that! If you didn't cheat, we wouldn't even be here now!" Sasha yelled. People had started to look at them.

"Sasha, you doing too much."

"Fuck doing too much. You cheated on me with my best friend! You are in a relationship with her! If you ask me, I'm doing enough. I could be taking you for everything you have! You and your bitch can kiss my ass!" Sasha yelled as she got up from her seat. She gathered up the bags that she had, and made a bee-line for the exit. Brandon sat for a couple of moments until he decided to chase after her. She had gotten pretty far by the time he made it to her. She was already putting the bags in her trunk when he approached her.

"Sasha, stop acting like a child and let's talk this out." Brandon said when he approached her.

"Fuck you, Brandon!" She jumped into the driver seat and started her car without letting it warm up.

"Sasha!" Brandon yelled through the window. Sasha drove out of the parking spot with tires screeching. There was a car coming out of lane. Neither one saw each other, and Sasha t-boned the other car. Brandon's heart dropped to the pits of his stomach. He ran to Sasha's car with his heart pounding.

"Sasha!" Brandon yelled when he got to her car. Her airbag had deployed, and she was pressed against the seat. She moved her head slightly, looking to the sound of Brandon's voice. When their eyes met, Sasha had tears in her eyes. People began to run over to the accident.

"Brandon, help me. I'm pregnant," Sasha managed to say before her eyes rolled to the back of her head.

"Somebody help. Call 911!" Brandon screamed as he tried to open her car door. The window on the passenger side had broken on impact, and that's how they were able to talk.

His heart was pounding in his chest as he tried to climb in to help Sasha. Brandon heard the sirens in the distance, but he needed to help her now.

Chapter Fifteen

Though I'm missing you
I'll find a way to get through
Living without you
'Cause you were my sister, my strength, and my pride
Only God may know why, still I will get by

The dark clouds that were overhead were a replica of everyone's mood. It was pouring, but the people in attendance were safely shielded by a white tent that could hold at least a hundred people. There was not a dry eye at the burial site, and the song that was playing didn't help. Amekia, Jade, and Sasha stood by the casket that held Carmen. She looked beautiful in a white dress. Her hair was in ringlet curls, and the funeral home did her justice with her make-up. Mrs. Bowden and Carmen's sister—Ashlyn—were inconsolable and almost fainted when they arrived at the burial site. Flowers adorned Carmen's white and gold casket.

A week ago, the same day that Sasha was in the car accident, Amekia had gotten a phone call from a distraught Ashlyn. She was too hysterical, and Amekia couldn't understand what was going on. She did get bits and pieces, and the only thing that Amekia was able to put together was: Carmen and gone. Amekia didn't want to think the worst, so she dropped what she was doing and headed over to Mrs. Bowden's house. She knew what she heard from Ashlyn was right. There was an ambulance, fire truck, and police car sitting out front of the house. There was caution tape around the perimeter of the yard, stopping people from walking past. Mrs. Bowden and Ashlyn were in the yard, holding onto each other, and Amekia said: 'Fuck the tape', and went under. She rushed over to the two women and hugged them, causing instant tears to fall from her eyes. Carmen's body was still in the house, and the authorities were waiting for the coroner to come.

"What the fuck happened?" Amekia cried.

"Zaquan, her nurse, came over to let her know that she was no longer gonna be his patient anymore because she was healed. I was in the kitchen fixing lunch and he asked if he could go see her. I thought that she was still sleeping and I told him that he could. When he entered the room, he knew instantly that something was wrong. Her lips had a blue tint to them and she was cold to his touch. He yelled for me to dial 911 and I ran to the room. My baby is gone and I knew in my heart that she had a habit with those damn pills, yet I turned a blind eye to the issue. I didn't want to admit it!" Mrs. Bowden yelled.

"Mama, don't put the blame on yourself," Ashlyn replied.

"She overdosed and I did nothing to prevent it! It is my fault, Ashlyn."

"No, it's not, Mrs. Bowden," Amekia said. She hated that Mrs. Bowden felt like it was her fault. Carmen was her best friend, and she had to admit that Carmen was the one to blame. Every one of them had issues they had to deal with but never thought about becoming hooked to any type of drugs to deal with their issues. The corner had arrived fifteen minutes after Amekia did. Amekia tried to get Ashlyn and Mrs. Bowden to move away from the front of the house. Nothing that Amekia did made them move. She wanted to break down and cry, but she needed to make sure that she had a clear head to deal with Mrs. Bowden and Ashlyn. As the coroner came out of the house, both Ashlyn and Mrs. Bowden fell to the ground, shrieking. The crowd that was on the opposite side of the tape looked on in horror. Some

showed sympathy and had tears in their eyes as well. Amekia watched in horror as her friend of over twenty years was laying in a body bag. Her body shook as she joined her best friend's mother and sister on the ground.

How sweet were the losses to spare?
But I'll wait for the day
When I'll see you again, see you again

Sasha leaned against Nas as she watched the casket get lowered into the ground. She was glad she survived the crash, and she had left the whole ordeal just bruised up, but she would have never guessed that her best friend would be gone. The oversized dark sunglasses that she had over her eyes shielded the redness and puffiness. She had been crying since the day she found out Carmen died. She wished, just like everyone else had, that Carmen had reached out to them to help her with her problem. No one would have turned a blind eye, but Carmen chose to stay silent.

When Sasha had gotten to the hospital, she was conscious and made sure to tell them that she was pregnant. Brandon stayed by her side until the doctors said that she was okay. He thought if they hadn't been arguing heatedly, the accident wouldn't have happened. He didn't know how he would have dealt with telling his kids that their mother passed because she was mad over something so silly. In the moment that they were running tests to make sure that she and the baby were okay, he decided that he was going to just agree to the spousal support. It wasn't enough for them to argue over and put her life in jeopardy. Brandon was sticking around the hospital because he needed to know if the baby she was carrying was his or not. Both were relieved when the doctor told her how far along she was because Nas was actually the father of the baby.

One by one, family and friends walked up to the hole in the ground, and everyone threw their white roses on top of Carmen's casket as it was being lowered. Jade, Amekia, and Sasha waited until everybody else went as they walked hand in hand up to the hole. Their sobbing was of true heartbreak, as they let their roses go at the same time. Even though Amekia and Sasha weren't feeling each other, they put their differences aside and held each other and cried. Timothy, Nas, and Brandon looked on, and their hearts broke for their girls. They each knew how their bond was with Carmen, and they knew that they had to be there to support them. The three of them stayed at the burial site for hours, even after she was lowered. The rain had stopped. The women sat in the front row of seats, just looking at the hole. Timothy, Brandon, and Nas sat in the last row, waiting patiently until the women were ready to leave.

The sun was gone by the time the women were ready to leave. With heavy hearts, they went home unsure of how they would live day to day without their best friend.

Chapter Sixteen

One Year Later

(Epilogue)

"Alexis and Aliana, go and tell Nas to come out down and help me with this damn table!" Sasha yelled to her daughters. She was setting up to have a memorial for Carmen at her house, and Nas promised to help. She had done all of the cooking for the event, but the folded picnic table that she was trying to assemble in her dining room was being a pain in her ass. Four months prior to the memorial, Sasha gave birth to Nas Jr. He was the perfect baby, and Nas could never leave him alone. Currently, Jr. was supposed to be napping but if Sasha had to place a bet, she knew that she would win. She knew that Nas was sitting in his son's room, watching him nap.

"Yeah, babe?" Nas said.

"Can you let Jr. nap on his own please? You were supposed to be helping with shit and here I am sweating and doing it by myself." Sasha whined.

"I'm sorry, love. What do you need me to do?" Nas asked while placing a kiss on Sasha's forehead.

"I need you to finish opening this table, put the food on top, and let me shower and get dressed."

"Okay, I got you. Let me just go check on Jr. right quick."

"Nas! You have the baby monitor on your hip. If he wakes up, you will hear him. He is fine. Just do what I asked, please?"

Nas nodded as Sasha walked away. She immediately jumped in the shower. People were going to arrive soon, and she wanted to at least be presentable. She rushed her shower. When she got out, she slipped on jeans, a fitted shirt that had Carmen's face on it, together with socks and slides. Over the past year, Sasha and Amekia had decided to be cordial with each other. After Carmen's death, they realized that even though they presently weren't cool, they could at least be civil in each other's presence. Sasha would never forget the unforgivable betrayal and secrets both Brandon and Amekia held, but it was time for her to heal and enjoy her relationship that she had with Nas. She owed that much to herself.

When she was done getting dressed, she made her way downstairs and was happy to see that Ashlyn and Mrs. Bowden were the first to arrive. They were rocking the same shirt that Sasha was wearing. Everybody at the memorial would be wearing the same shirt as well. Soon after, Jade and Timothy entered, followed by Brandon and a very pregnant Amekia. She was due in a month, and was giving Brandon a boy.

At the dinner table, everyone shared stories of Carmen in remembrance. Laughter was shared, and so were tears. Above all else, they all knew that Carmen was with every one of them; they knew she dwelled in their lives, and they couldn't have been happier. Dinner took hours to complete because where one story ended, another one began.

"Okay y'all, we gotta release the balloons," Sasha called out, getting everyone's attention. Nas walked into the garage while everyone gathered their coats to put on. Sasha had stored over a hundred pink balloons in the garage. Instead of making several trips, Nas had Timothy and Brandon to help him. Once everyone was bundled up, they walked into Sasha's back yard.

"Three! Two! One! We miss and love you, Carmen!" They shouted in unison and let the balloons go, with tears in their eyes. While Carmen's body was gone physically, at that moment they all felt her spirit.

"Long live Carmen!" Amekia shouted.

The End

Submission Guideline

Submit the first three chapters of your completed manuscript to ldpsubmissions@gmail.com, subject line: Your book's title. The manuscript must be in a .doc file and sent as an attachment. Document should be in Times New Roman, double spaced and in size 12 font. Also, provide your synopsis and full contact information. If sending multiple submissions, they must each be in a separate email.

Have a story but no way to send it electronically? You can still submit to LDP/Ca$h Presents. Send in the first three chapters, written or typed, of your completed manuscript to:

LDP: Submissions Dept
Po Box 944
Stockbridge, Ga 30281

DO NOT send original manuscript. Must be a duplicate.

Provide your synopsis and a cover letter containing your full contact information.

Thanks for considering LDP and Ca$h Presents.

NEW RELEASE

FRIEND OR FOE 3 by MIMI

Coming Soon from Lock Down Publications/Ca$h Presents

BLOOD OF A BOSS **VI**

SHADOWS OF THE GAME II

TRAP BASTARD II

By **Askari**

LOYAL TO THE GAME **IV**

By **T.J. & Jelissa**

IF TRUE SAVAGE **VIII**

MIDNIGHT CARTEL IV

DOPE BOY MAGIC IV

CITY OF KINGZ III

By **Chris Green**

BLAST FOR ME **III**

A SAVAGE DOPEBOY III

CUTTHROAT MAFIA III

DUFFLE BAG CARTEL VII

HEARTLESS GOON VI

By **Ghost**

A HUSTLER'S DECEIT III

KILL ZONE II

BAE BELONGS TO ME III

A DOPE BOY'S QUEEN III

By **Aryanna**

COKE KINGS V

KING OF THE TRAP III

By **T.J. Edwards**

GORILLAZ IN THE BAY V

3X KRAZY III

De'Kari

KINGPIN KILLAZ IV

STREET KINGS III

PAID IN BLOOD III

CARTEL KILLAZ IV

DOPE GODS III

Hood Rich

SINS OF A HUSTLA II

ASAD

RICH $AVAGE II

By Troublesome

YAYO V

Bred In The Game 2

S. Allen

CREAM III

By Yolanda Moore

SON OF A DOPE FIEND III

HEAVEN GOT A GHETTO II

By Renta

LOYALTY AIN'T PROMISED III

By Keith Williams

I'M NOTHING WITHOUT HIS LOVE II

SINS OF A THUG II

TO THE THUG I LOVED BEFORE II

By Monet Dragun

QUIET MONEY IV

EXTENDED CLIP III

THUG LIFE IV

By **Trai'Quan**

THE STREETS MADE ME III

By **Larry D. Wright**

IF YOU CROSS ME ONCE II

By **Anthony Fields**

THE STREETS WILL NEVER CLOSE II

By K'ajji

HARD AND RUTHLESS III

Von Diesel

KILLA KOUNTY II

By Khufu

MOBBED UP III

By King Rio

MONEY GAME II

By Smoove Dolla

Available Now

RESTRAINING ORDER **I & II**

By **CA$H & Coffee**

LOVE KNOWS NO BOUNDARIES **I II & III**

By **Coffee**

RAISED AS A GOON I, II, III & IV

BRED BY THE SLUMS I, II, III

BLAST FOR ME I & II

ROTTEN TO THE CORE I II III

A BRONX TALE I, II, III

DUFFLE BAG CARTEL I II III IV V VI

HEARTLESS GOON I II III IV V

A SAVAGE DOPEBOY I II

DRUG LORDS I II III

CUTTHROAT MAFIA I II

KING OF THE TRENCHES

By **Ghost**

LAY IT DOWN **I & II**

LAST OF A DYING BREED I II

BLOOD STAINS OF A SHOTTA I & II III

By **Jamaica**

LOYAL TO THE GAME I II III

LIFE OF SIN I, II III

By **TJ & Jelissa**

BLOODY COMMAS I & II

SKI MASK CARTEL I II & III

KING OF NEW YORK I II,III IV V

RISE TO POWER I II III

COKE KINGS I II III IV

BORN HEARTLESS I II III IV

KING OF THE TRAP I II

By **T.J. Edwards**

IF LOVING HIM IS WRONG…I & II

LOVE ME EVEN WHEN IT HURTS I II III

By **Jelissa**

WHEN THE STREETS CLAP BACK I & II III

THE HEART OF A SAVAGE I II III

By **Jibril Williams**

A DISTINGUISHED THUG STOLE MY HEART I II & III

LOVE SHOULDN'T HURT I II III IV

RENEGADE BOYS I II III IV

PAID IN KARMA I II III

SAVAGE STORMS I II

AN UNFORESEEN LOVE

By **Meesha**

A GANGSTER'S CODE I &, II III

A GANGSTER'S SYN I II III

THE SAVAGE LIFE I II III

CHAINED TO THE STREETS I II III

BLOOD ON THE MONEY I II III

By J-Blunt

PUSH IT TO THE LIMIT

By **Bre' Hayes**

BLOOD OF A BOSS **I, II, III, IV, V**

SHADOWS OF THE GAME

TRAP BASTARD

By **Askari**

THE STREETS BLEED MURDER **I, II & III**

THE HEART OF A GANGSTA I II& III

By **Jerry Jackson**

CUM FOR ME I II III IV V VI VII

An **LDP Erotica Collaboration**

BRIDE OF A HUSTLA **I II & II**

THE FETTI GIRLS **I, II& III**

CORRUPTED BY A GANGSTA I, II III, IV

BLINDED BY HIS LOVE

THE PRICE YOU PAY FOR LOVE I, II ,III

DOPE GIRL MAGIC I II III

By **Destiny Skai**

WHEN A GOOD GIRL GOES BAD

By **Adrienne**

THE COST OF LOYALTY I II III

By Kweli

A GANGSTER'S REVENGE **I II III & IV**

THE BOSS MAN'S DAUGHTERS I II III IV V

A SAVAGE LOVE **I & II**

BAE BELONGS TO ME I II

A HUSTLER'S DECEIT I, II, III

WHAT BAD BITCHES DO I, II, III

SOUL OF A MONSTER I II III

KILL ZONE

A DOPE BOY'S QUEEN I II

By **Aryanna**

A KINGPIN'S AMBITON

A KINGPIN'S AMBITION **II**

I MURDER FOR THE DOUGH

By **Ambitious**

TRUE SAVAGE I II III IV V VI VII

DOPE BOY MAGIC I, II, III

MIDNIGHT CARTEL I II III

CITY OF KINGZ I II

By **Chris Green**

A DOPEBOY'S PRAYER

By **Eddie "Wolf" Lee**

THE KING CARTEL **I, II & III**

By **Frank Gresham**

THESE NIGGAS AIN'T LOYAL **I, II & III**

By **Nikki Tee**

GANGSTA SHYT **I II &III**

By **CATO**

THE ULTIMATE BETRAYAL

By **Phoenix**

BOSS'N UP **I , II & III**

By **Royal Nicole**

I LOVE YOU TO DEATH

By **Destiny J**

I RIDE FOR MY HITTA

I STILL RIDE FOR MY HITTA

By **Misty Holt**

LOVE & CHASIN' PAPER

By **Qay Crockett**

TO DIE IN VAIN

SINS OF A HUSTLA

By **ASAD**

BROOKLYN HUSTLAZ

By **Boogsy Morina**

BROOKLYN ON LOCK I & II

By **Sonovia**

GANGSTA CITY

By **Teddy Duke**

A DRUG KING AND HIS DIAMOND I & II III

A DOPEMAN'S RICHES

HER MAN, MINE'S TOO I, II

CASH MONEY HO'S

THE WIFEY I USED TO BE I II

By Nicole Goosby

TRAPHOUSE KING **I II & III**

KINGPIN KILLAZ I II III

STREET KINGS I II

PAID IN BLOOD **I II**

CARTEL KILLAZ I II III

DOPE GODS I II

By **Hood Rich**

LIPSTICK KILLAH **I, II, III**

CRIME OF PASSION I II & III

FRIEND OR FOE I II III

By **Mimi**

STEADY MOBBN' **I, II, III**

THE STREETS STAINED MY SOUL I II

By **Marcellus Allen**

WHO SHOT YA **I, II, III**

SON OF A DOPE FIEND I II

HEAVEN GOT A GHETTO

Renta

GORILLAZ IN THE BAY **I II III IV**

TEARS OF A GANGSTA I II

3X KRAZY I II

DE'KARI

TRIGGADALE I II III

Elijah R. Freeman

GOD BLESS THE TRAPPERS I, II, III

THESE SCANDALOUS STREETS I, II, III

FEAR MY GANGSTA I, II, III IV, V

THESE STREETS DON'T LOVE NOBODY I, II

BURY ME A G I, II, III, IV, V

A GANGSTA'S EMPIRE I, II, III, IV

THE DOPEMAN'S BODYGAURD I II

THE REALEST KILLAZ I II III

THE LAST OF THE OGS I II III

Tranay Adams

THE STREETS ARE CALLING

Duquie Wilson

MARRIED TO A BOSS I II III

By Destiny Skai & Chris Green

KINGZ OF THE GAME I II III IV V

Playa Ray

SLAUGHTER GANG I II III

RUTHLESS HEART I II III

By Willie Slaughter

FUK SHYT

By Blakk Diamond

DON'T F#CK WITH MY HEART I II

By Linnea

ADDICTED TO THE DRAMA I II III

IN THE ARM OF HIS BOSS II

By Jamila

YAYO I II III IV

A SHOOTER'S AMBITION I II

BRED IN THE GAME

By S. Allen

TRAP GOD I II III

RICH $AVAGE

By Troublesome

FOREVER GANGSTA

GLOCKS ON SATIN SHEETS I II

By Adrian Dulan

TOE TAGZ I II III

LEVELS TO THIS SHYT I II

By Ah'Million

KINGPIN DREAMS I II III

By Paper Boi Rari

CONFESSIONS OF A GANGSTA I II III

By Nicholas Lock

I'M NOTHING WITHOUT HIS LOVE

SINS OF A THUG

TO THE THUG I LOVED BEFORE

By Monet Dragun

CAUGHT UP IN THE LIFE I II III

By Robert Baptiste

NEW TO THE GAME I II III

MONEY, MURDER & MEMORIES I II III

By **Malik D. Rice**

LIFE OF A SAVAGE I II III

A GANGSTA'S QUR'AN I II III

MURDA SEASON I II III

GANGLAND CARTEL I II III

CHI'RAQ GANGSTAS I II III

KILLERS ON ELM STREET I II III

JACK BOYZ N DA BRONX I II III

A DOPEBOY'S DREAM

By **Romell Tukes**

LOYALTY AIN'T PROMISED I II

By Keith Williams

QUIET MONEY I II III

THUG LIFE I II III

EXTENDED CLIP I II

By **Trai'Quan**

THE STREETS MADE ME I II

By **Larry D. Wright**

THE ULTIMATE SACRIFICE I, II, III, IV, V, VI

KHADIFI

IF YOU CROSS ME ONCE

ANGEL I II

IN THE BLINK OF AN EYE

By **Anthony Fields**

THE LIFE OF A HOOD STAR

By Ca$h & Rashia Wilson

THE STREETS WILL NEVER CLOSE

By K'ajji

CREAM I II

By Yolanda Moore

NIGHTMARES OF A HUSTLA I II III

By King Dream

CONCRETE KILLA I II

By Kingpen

HARD AND RUTHLESS I II

MOB TOWN 251

By Von Diesel

GHOST MOB

Stilloan Robinson

MOB TIES I II

By SayNoMore

BODYMORE MURDERLAND I II III

By Delmont Player

FOR THE LOVE OF A BOSS

By C. D. Blue

MOBBED UP I II

By King Rio

KILLA KOUNTY

By Khufu

MONEY GAME II

By Smoove Dolla

BOOKS BY LDP'S CEO, CA$H

TRUST IN NO MAN

TRUST IN NO MAN 2

TRUST IN NO MAN 3

BONDED BY BLOOD

SHORTY GOT A THUG

THUGS CRY

THUGS CRY 2

THUGS CRY 3

TRUST NO BITCH

TRUST NO BITCH 2

TRUST NO BITCH 3

TIL MY CASKET DROPS

RESTRAINING ORDER

RESTRAINING ORDER 2

IN LOVE WITH A CONVICT

LIFE OF A HOOD STAR

CPSIA information can be obtained
at www.ICGtesting.com
Printed in the USA
LVHW081443211121
704028LV00011B/1220